Verb Chart

Quenya-English

English-Quenya

v. 2.0

http://www. ambar-eldaron.com

ISBN 978-1508801795

Ambar Eldaron

presents its conjugation Quenya verb Chart v. 2.0

In this booklet, we have gathered all the known verbs, so 388 verbs.

We have conjugated them following the grammar standards, including the last indications of VT49.

Some verbs are problematic. We have done as well as we could given our knowledge. The o-verbs are no more valid in mature Quenya, but we have cited two of them with question mark (?).

You'll find some derived verbs which seem particularly useful. They are marked by a star (*).

The attested forms are indicated with **bold** letters.

Some verbs are incomplete. Until now we don't have other information concerning them. The correspondant cells are empty.

In order to facilitate the searching in the English-Quenya section, we have listed several times the same verb, following its different meanings.

Quenya- English

verbal stem	definition	infinitive	present	aoriste	future	past	perfect	imperative	active pp.	passive pp.	gerund
ahya-	change	ahya	ahyëa	ahya	ahyuva	**ahyanë**	ahánië, háhië	á ahya	ahyala	ahyaina	ahië
airita-	hallow	airita	airitëa	airita	airituva	**airitánë**	ahairitië	á airita	airitala	airitaina	airitië
aista-	bless, dread	aista	aistëa	aista	aistuva	aistanë	ahaistië	á aista	aistala	**aistana**	aistië
al-	thrive	alë	ála	alë, ali-	aluva	allë	álië, alálië	á alë	álala	alda	alië
ala-	thrive	ala	alëa	ala	aluva	alanë	álië, alálië	á ala	alala	alaina	alië
alála-	continually grow	alála	alálëa	alála	aláluva	alálanë	álië, alálië	á alála	alálala	alálaina	alálië
alta-	dread	alta	altëa	alta	altuva	altanë	áltië, aláltië	á alta	altala	altaina	altië
*amavil-	fly up	amavilë	amáwila	amavilë, amavili-	amaviluva	amavillë	ahamavilië	á amavilë	amavilala	amavilda	amavilië
*amawil-	fly up	amawilë	amáwila	amawilë, amawili-	amawiluva	amawillë	ahamiwilië	á amawilë	amawilala	amawilda	amawilië
amorta-	heave	amorta	amortëa	amorta	amortuva	amortanë	ámortië, amámortië	á amorta	**amortala**	amortaina	amortië
amu-	raise	amo	ámua	amwë, amwi-	amúva	amunë	ámië, amámië	á amo	amúla	amuina	amië
anta-	give	anta	antëa	anta	antuva	antanë, ánë	ántië, anántië	á anta	antala	antaina	antië
ap-	affect, concern	apë	ápa	**apë, api-**	apuva	ampë	ápië, apápië	á apë	ápala	ápina	apië

verbal stem	definition	infinitive	present	aoriste	future	past	perfect	imperative	active pp.	passive pp.	gerund
appa-	touch (literally)	appa	appëa	appa	appuva	appanë	áppië, appápië	á appa	appala	appaina	appië
apsene-	forgive (+dative of person forgiven)	apsenë	apsénëa	apsenë	apsenuva	apsennë	apsénië	á apsenë	apsénala	apseneina	apsenië
arca-	pray	arca	arcëa	arca	arcuva	arcanë	árcië	á arca	arcala	arcaina	arcië
ascat-	break asunder	ascatë	ascáta	ascatë, ascati-	ascatuva	**ascantë**	ascátië	á ascatë	ascatala	ascatina	ascatië
*atacar-	take vengeance	altacarë	altacára	altacarë, altacari-	altacaruva	altacarnë	ahalatacárië	á altacarë	altacárala	altacarma	altacarië
atalta-	collapse, fall in	atalta	ataltëa	atalta	ataltuva	**ataltanë**	atáltië	á atalta	ataltala	ataltaina	ataltië
auta- /1	leave, go away	auta	autëa	auta	autuva	**anwë, vánë**	avánië	á auta	autala	vanwa	autië
auta- /2	leave physically	auta	autëa	auta	autuva	**oantë**	oantië	á auta	autala	vanwa	autië
auta- /3	invent, originate	auta	autëa	auta	autuva	**autanë**	avánië	á auta	autala	vanwa	autië
áva-	refuse, prohibit	áva	ávëa	ava	avuva	**avanë**	ávië, avávië	**áva**	avala	avaina	avië
avalatya-	close	avalatya	avalatyëa	avalatya	avalatyuva	avalatyanë	ávalátië	á avalatya	avalatyala	avalatyaina	avalatië
*avalerya-	bind, deprive of liberty	avalerya	avaleryëa	avalerya	avaleryuva	avalernë	ávalérië	á avalerya	avaleryala	avaleryaina	avalerië
avaquet-	refuse, say no	avaquetë	avaquéta	avaquetë, avaqueti-	avaquetuva	avaquetë	avaquetië	á avaquetë	avaquétala	avaquetina	avaquetië

verbal stem	definition	infinitive	present	aoriste	future	past	perfect	imperative	active pp.	passive pp.	gerund
avatyar- +ablatif	forgive	avatyarë	avatyara	avatyarë	avatyaruva	avatyaranë	avatyarië	á avatyarë, ávatyarë	avatyarala	avatyarna	avatyarië
caita-	lie (horizontally)	caita	caitëa	caita	caituva	cainë, cëante	acaitië	á caita	caitala	caitaina	caitië
cal-	shine	calë	cála	calë, cali-	caluva	callë	acálië	á calë	cálala	calda	calië
calpa-	draw water	calpa	calpëa	calpa	calpuva	calpanë	acalpië	á calpa	calpala	calpaina	calpië
calta-	kindle (set light to)	calta	caltëa	calta	caltuva	caltanë	acaltië	á calta	caltala	caltaina	caltië
calya-	illuminate-	calya	calyëa	calya	calyuva	calyanë	acálië	á calya	calyala	calyaina	calië
cam-	receive	camë	cáma	camë, cami-	camuva	camnë	cámië	á camë	camala	camaina	camië
camta-	accommodate	camta	camtëa	camta	camtuva	camtanë	acámië	á camta	camtala	camtaina	camtië
can-	command, order	canë	cána	canë, cani-	canuva	cannë	acánië	á canë	cánala	canna	canië
cap-	jump	capë	cápa	capë, capi-	capuva	campë	acápië	á capë	cápala	cápina	capië
car-	build	carë	cára	carë, cari-	caruva	carnë	cárië, acárië	á carë	cárala	carna, carina	carië
cen-	make	cenë	céna	cenë, ceni-	cenuva	cennë	ecénië	á cena	cénala	cenna	cenië
cenda-	watch	cenda	cendëa	cenda	cenduva	cendanë	ecendië	á cenda	cendala	cendaina	cendië

verbal stem	definition	infinitive	present	aoriste	future	past	perfect	imperative	active pp.	passive pp.	gerund
*cil-	choose	cilë	cila	cilë, cil-	ciluva	cillë	icilië	á cilë	cilala	cilda	cilië
*cilta-	divide, cleave	cilta	ciltëa	cilta	ciltuva	ciltanë	iciltië	á cilta	ciltala	ciltaina	ciltië
cim-	heed	cimë	címa	cimë, cimi-	cimuva	cimnë	icímië	á cimë	címala	cimna	cimië
círa-	sail	círa	círëa	círa	círuva	círanë	icirië	á círa	círala	círaina	círië
col-	bear	colë	cóla	colë, coli-	coluva	collë	ocólië	á colë	cólala	**colla**	colië
costa-	quarrel	costa	costëa	costa	costuva	costanë	ocostië	á costa	costala	costaina	costië
*cuil-	live	cuilë	cuila	cuilë, cuili-	cuiluva	cuillë	ucuilië	á cuilë	cuilala	cuilda	cuilië
cúna-	bend (intr.)	cúna	cúnëa	cúna	cúnuva	cúnanë	ucúnië	á cúna	cúnala	cúnaina	cunië
ëa	be, exist	ëa		ëa		engë		ëa!			
eccoita-	wake up	eccoita	eccoitëa	eccoita	eccoituva	eccoitanë	eccoitië	á eccoita	eccoitala	eccoitaina	eccoitië
effir-	expire, die	effírë	effíra	effírë	effíruva	effírnë	effírië	á effírë	effírala	effírna	**effírië**
empanya-	plant	empanya	empanyëa	empanya	empanyuva	**empannë**	empánië	á empanya	empanyala	empanyaina	empanië
enquat-	refill	enquatë	enquáta	enquatë, enquati-	**enquantuva**	enquantë	enquátië	á enquatë	enquátala	enquátina	enquatië

verbal stem	definition	infinitive	present	aoriste	future	past	perfect	imperative	active pp.	passive pp.	gerund
entul-	return, come back	entulë	entúla	entulë, entuli-	entuluva	entullë	entúlië	á entulë	entulala	entulda	entulië
envinyata-	heal, renew	envinyata	envinyatëa	envinyata	envinyatuva	envinyatánë	envinyatië	á envinyata	envinyatála	envinyanta	envinyatië
enyal-	renew	enyalë	enyála	enyalë, enyali-	enyaluva	enyallë	enayálië	á enyala	enyalala	enyalla	enyalië
er-	remain	erë	éra	erë, eri-	eruva	ernë	ehernië	á erë	erala	erma	erië
erca-	prick	erca	ercëa	erca	ercuva	ercanë	ercië, erercië	á erca	ercala	ercaina	ercië
esta-	name	esta	estëa	esta	estuva	estanë	ehestië, estië	á esta	estala	estaina	estië
etelehta-	deliver (save)	etelehta	etelehtëa	etelehta	etelehtuva	etelehtanë	etelehtië	á etelehta	etelehtala	etelehtaina	etelehtië
*etementa-	ban, drive out	etementa	etementëa	etementa	etementuva	etementanë	etetementië, etementië	á etementa	etementala	etementaina	etementië
eterúna-	deliver	eterúna	aterúnëa	eterúna	eterúnuva	eterúnanë	eterúnië	á eterúna	eterúnala	eterúnaina	eterúnië
etrúna-	deliver	eterúna	aterúnëa	eterúna	eterúnuva	eterúnanë	etrúnië	á eterúna	eterúnala	eterúnaina	eterúnië
etsat-	distribute in even portions	etsatë	etsáta	etsatë, etsati-	etsatuva	etsantë	etsatië	á etsatë	etsátala	etsatina	etsatië
ettul-	come forth	ettulë	ettíla	ettulë, ettuli-	ettuluva	ettullë	ettulië	á ettulë	ettulala	ettulaina	ettulië
faina-	emit light	faina	fainëa	faina	fainuva	fainanë	afainië	á faina	fainala	fainaina	fainië

verbal stem	definition	infinitive	present	aoriste	future	past	perfect	imperative	active pp.	passive pp.	gerund
falasta-	foam	falasta	falastëa	falasta	falastuva	falastanë	afálastië	á falasta	**falastala**	falastaina	falastië
fanta-	veil, cloak	fanta	fantëa	fanta	fantuva	fantanë	afantië	á fanta	fantala	fantaina	fantië
farya-	emit light	farya	faryëa	farya	faryuva	**farnë**	afárië	á farya	faryala	faryaina,	farië
fasta-	tangle	fasta	fastëa	fasta	fastuva	fastanë	afastië	á fasta	fastala	fastaina	fastië
fauta-	snow	fautë	fauta	fauta	fautuva	fautë	afautië	á fautë	fautala	fautina	fautië
fel-	feel	felë	féla	felë, feli-	feluva	fellë	efelië	á felë	félala	felda	felië
feuya-	feel disgust at, abhor	feuya	feuyëa	feuya	feuyuva	feuyanë	eféwië	á feuya	feuyala	feuyaina	feuië
fifíru-	slowly fade away	fifíro	fifírua	fifírui	fifíriva	fifírunë	iffírië	á fifíro	**fifírula**	fifíruina	fifírië
fir-	die, fade	firë	fíra	**firë, firi-**	fíruva	fírnë	ifírië, **firië**	á firë	fírala	fírna	firië
fur-	conceal, lie	furë	fúra	furë, furi-	furuva	furnë	ufúrië	á furë	furala	furna	furië
haca-	squat	haca	hácëa	haca	hacuva	hacanë	ahácië	á haca	hácala	hacaina	hacië
halta-	leap	halta	haltëa	halta	haltuva	haltanë	ahaltië	á halta	haltala	haltaina	haltië
halya-	conceal, screen from the light	halya	halyëa	halya	halyuva	halyanë	ahálië	á halya	halyala	halyaina	halië

verbal stem	definition	infinitive	present	aoriste	future	past	perfect	imperative	active pp.	passive pp.	gerund
ham-	sit	hamë	háma	**hamë, hami-**	hamuva	hamnë	ahámië	á hamë	hámala	hamma	hamië
ham-	judge	hamë	háma	**hamë, hami-**	hamuva	hamnë	ahámië	á hamë	hámala	hamma	hamië
hanta-	thank, give thanks	hanta	hantëa	hanta	hantuva	hantanë	ahantië	á hanta	hantala	hantaina	hantië
hanya-	understand, know about	hanya	hanyëa	hanya	hanyuva	hanyanë	ahánië	á hanya	haryala	hanyaina	hanië
har-	sit	harë	**hára**	harë, hari-	haruva	**handë**	ahárië	á harë	hárala	harna	harië
harna-	wound	harna	harnëa	harna	harnuva	harnanë	aharnië	á harna	harnala	**harna**	harnië
harya-	have, possess	harya	haryëa	harya	haryuva	harnë	ahárië	á harya	tévala	haryaina	harië
hasta-	mar	hasta	hastëa	hasta	hastuva	hastanë	ahastië	á hasta	hastala	**hastaina**	hastië
hat-	break asunder	hatë	háta	hatë, hati-	hatuva	**hantë**	ahátië	á hatë	hátala	hátina	hatië
hauta-	cease, take rest, stop	hauta	hautëa	hauta	hautuva	hautanë	ahautië	á hauta	hautala	hautaina	hautië
hehta-	abandon, put aside	hehta	hehtëa	hehta	hehtuva	**hehtanë**	ehehtië	á hehta	hehtala	hehtaina	hehtië
hel-	frost	helë	héla	helë, heli-	heluva	hellë	ehelië	á helë	hélala	helda	helië
hep-	hold	hepë	hépa	hepë, hepi-	hepuva	hempë	ehempië	á hepë	hépela	hepina	hepië

verbal stem	definition	infinitive	present	aoriste	future	past	perfect	imperative	active pp.	passive pp.	gerund
heru-	rule	hero	hérua	herwë, herwi-	herúva	herunë	ehérië	á hero	herúla	heruina	herië
hilya-	follow	hilya	hilyëa	hilya	hilyuva	hilyanë	ihlië	á hilya	hilyala	hilyaina	hilië
himya-	abide by, stick, adhere	himya	himyëa	himya	himyuva	himyanë	ihímië	á himya	himyala	himyaina	himië
hir-	find	hirë	híra	hirë, hiri-	**hiruva**	hirnë	ihírië	á hirë	hirala	hirna	hirië
huita-	wink, hint	huita	huitëa	huita	huituva	huitanë	uhuitië	á huita	huitala	huitina	huitië
hlapu-	blow, fly or stream in the wond	hlapo	hlápua	hlapui	hlapúva	hlapunë	ahlápië	á hlapo	**hlápula**	hlapuina	hlapië
hlar-	hear	hlarë	hlára	hlarë, hlari-	**hlaruva**	hlarnë	ahlárië	á hlarë	hlárala	hlarna	hlarië
hlussa-	whisper	hlussa	hlussëa	hlussa	hlussuva	hlussanë	uhlussië	á hlussa	hlussala	hlussaina	hlussië
hóciri-	cut off	hócirë	**hócira**	**hócirë**	hóciruva	**hócirnë**	ohócirië	á hócirë	hócirila	hócirina	hócirië
horta-	speed, urge	horta	hortëa	horta	hortuva	hortanë	ohortië	á horta	hortala	hortaina	hortië
horya-	have an impulse, becompelled to do	horya	horyëa	horya	horyuva	hornë	ohórië	á horya	horyala	horyaina	horië
hosta-	gather, collect	hosta	hostëa	hosta	hostuva	hostanë	ohostië	á hosta	hostala	**hostaina**	hostie
hum-	not to do	humë	húma	**humë, humi-**	humuva	**húmë**	uhúmië	á huma	humala	humna	humië

verbal stem	definition	infinitive	present	aoriste	future	past	perfect	imperative	active pp.	passive pp.	gerund
húna-	howl	húna	húnëa	húna	húnuva	húnanë	uhúnië	á húna	húnala	húnaina	húnië
hur-	conceal, lie	hurë	húra	hurë, huri-	huruva	hurnë	uhúrië	á hurë	húrala	hurna	hurië
hwesta-	puff	hwesta	hwestëa	hwesta	hwestuva	hwestanë	ehwestië	á hwesta	hwestala	hwestaina	hwestië
hwinya-	swirl, girate	hwinya	hwinyëa	hwinya	hwinyuva	hwinnë	ihwínië	á hwinya	hwinyala	hwinyaina	hwinië-
hyam-	pray	hyamë	hyama	**hyamë, hyami-**	hyamuva	hyamnë	ahyámië	á hyama	hyamala	hyamna	hyamië
hyar-	cleave	hyarë	hyára	**hyarë, hyari-**	hyaruva	**hyandë**	ahyárië	á hyarë	hyárala	hyarna	hyarië
ilca-	gleam (white)	ilca	ilcëa	ilca	ilcuva	ilcanë	lilcië, ilcië	á ilca	**ilcala**	ilcaina	ilcië
intya-	guess, suppose	intya	intyëa	intya	intyuva	intyanë	inintië, intië	á intya	intyala	intyaina	intië
ista-	suppose	ista	istëa	**ista**	istuva	**sintë**	isintië, sintië	á ista	istala	istaina	istië
ita-	sparkle	ita	itëa	ita	ituva	itanë	ihitië, itië	á ita	itala	itaina	itië
laita-	bless	laita	laitëa	laita	**laituva**	laitanë	alaitië	**á laita**	laitala	laitaina	laitië
lala-	deny	lala	lálëa	lala	laluva	lalanë, lallë	alálië,	á lala	lalala	lalaina	lalië
lala-	laugh	lala	lálëa	lala	láluva	lalanë, landë	alálië	á lala	lálala	lalaina	lalië

verbal stem	definition	infinitive	present	aoriste	future	past	perfect	imperative	active pp.	passive pp.	gerund
lamya-	sound	lamya	lamya	lamya	lamyuva	lamnë	alámië	á lamya	lamyala	lamyaina	lamië
lanta-	fall	lanta	lantëa	lanta	lantuva	lantanë	alantië, lantië	á lanta	lantala	lantaina	lantië
lanya-	bound, enclose	lanya	lanyëa	lanya	lanyuva	lanyanë	alánië	á lanya	lanyala	lanyaina	lanië
lanya-	weave	lanya	lanyëa	lanya	lanyuva	lanyanë	alánië	á lanya	lanyala	lanyaina	lanië
lapsa-	lick (frequentative)	lapsa	lapsëa	lapsa	lapsuva	lapsanë	alapsië	á lapsa	lapsala	lapsaina	lapsië
laquet-	deny	laquetë	laqueta	laquetë, laqueti-	laquetuva	laquetë	alaquetië	á laquetë	laquétala	laquétina	laquetië
lara-	make flat	lara	larëa	lara	laruva	laranë	alarië	á lara	larala	laraina	larië
lasta-	listen	lasta	lastëa	lasta	lastuva	lastanë	alastië	á lasta	lastala	lastaina	lastië
latya-	open	latya	latyëa	latya	latyuva	latyanë	alátië	á latya	latyala	latyaina	latië
lauta-	warm	lauta	lautëa	lauta	lautuva	lautanë	alautië	á lauta	lautala	lautaina	lautië
lav-	allow	lave	láva	lavë, lavi-	lavuva	lávë	alávië	á lavë	lávala	lávina	lavië
lav-	lick	lave	láva	lavë, lavi-	lavuva	lávë	alávië	á lavë	lávala	lávina	lavië
lehta-	loose, slacken	lehta	lehtëa	lehta	lehtuva	lehtanë	elehtië	á lehta	lehtala	lehtaina	lehtië

verbal stem	definition	infinitive	present	aoriste	future	past	perfect	imperative	active pp.	passive pp.	gerund
lelta-	send	lelta	leltëa	lelta	leltuva	**leltanë**	eleltië	á lelta	leltala	leltaina	leltië
lelya-	go, proceed	lelya	lelyëa	lelya	lelyuva	**lendë**	elélië, lendië	á lelya	lelyala	lelyaina	lelië
lemya-	remain, tarry	lemya	lemyëa	lemya	lemyuva	lemyanë	elémië	á lemya	lemyala	lemyaina	lemië
lenca-	loose, slacken	lenca	lencëa	lenca	lencuva	lencanë	elencië	á lenca	lencala	lencaina	lencië
lenda-	linger	lenda	lendëa	lenda	lenduva	lendanë	elendië, **lendië**	á lenda	lendala	lendaina	lendië
lenna-	go	lenna	lennëa	lenna	lennuva	lennë	elennië	á lenna	lennala	lennaina	lennië
lenta	send	lenta	lentëa	lenta	lentuva	**lentanë**	elentië	á lenta	lentala	lentaina	lentië
lenu-	stretch	leno	lénua	lenwë, lenwi-	lenúva	lenunë	elénië	á leno	lenúla	lenuina	lenië
lepta-	pick up with fingers	lepta	leptëa	lepta	leptuva	leptanë	eleptië	á lepta	leptala	leptaina	leptië
lerta-	can, be free to do	lerta	lertëa	**lerta**	lertuva	lertanë	elertië	á lerta	lertala	lertaina	lertië
lerya-	release	lerya	leryëa	lerya	leryuva	leryanë	eléryë	á lerya	leryala	leryaina	lerië
lesta-	leave	lesta	lesteä	lesta	lestuva	**lendë**	elestië	á lesta	lestala	lestaina	lestië
lilta-	dance	lilta	liltëa	lilta	liltuva	liltanë	ililtië	á lilta	liltala	liltaina	liltië

verbal stem	definition	infinitive	present	aoriste	future	past	perfect	imperative	active pp.	passive pp.	gerund
linda-	sing	linda	lindëa	linda	linduva	lindanë	ilindië	á linda	lindala	lindaina	lindië
linga-	hang, dangle	linga	lingëa	linga	linguva	linganë	ilingië	á linga	lingala	lingaina	lingië
lir-	sing	lire	lira	**lirë, liri-**	liruva	lirnë	ilirië	á lire	lirala	lirna	lirië
locta-	sprout	locta	loctëa	locta	loctuva	loctanë	oloctië	á locta	loctala	loctaina	loctië
lohta-	sprout	lohta	lohtëa	lohta	lohtuva	lohtanë	olohtië	á lohta	lohtala	lohtaina	lohtië
lom-	hide	lomë	lóma	**lomë, lomi-**	lomuva	lomnë	olómië	á lomë	lómala	lomna	lomië
lor-	slumber	lorë	lóra	lorë, lori-	loruva	lornë	olórië	á lorë	lórala	lorna	lorië
lohta-	sprout	lohta	lohtëa	lohta	lohtuva	lohtanë	olohtië	á lohta	lohtala	lohtaina	lohtië
losta-	Bloom	losta	lostëa	losta	lostuva	lostanë	olostië	á losta	lostala	lostaina	lostië
luhta-	enchant	luhta	luhtëa	luhta	luhtuva	luhtanë	uluhtië	á luhta	luhtala	luhtaina	luhtië
luhta-	bow	luhta	luhtëa	luhta	luhtuva	luhtanë	uluhtië	á luhta	luhtala	luhtaina	luhtië
luita-	flood	luita	luitëa	luita	luituva	luitanë	uluitië	á luita	luitala	luitaina	luitië
lumna-	lie heavy	lumna	lumnëa	lumna	lumnuva	**luvë**	ulumnië	á lumna	lumnala	lumnaina	lumnië

verbal stem	definition	infinitive	present	aoriste	future	past	perfect	imperative	active pp.	passive pp.	gerund
lussa-	whisper	lus sa	lussëa	lussa	lussuva	lussanë	ulussië	á lussa	lussala	lussaina	lussië
lutta-	flow, float	lutta	luttëa	lutta	luttuva	luttanë	uluttië	á lutta	luttala	luttaina	luttië
lutu-	flow, float	luto	lútua	lutui	lutúva	lutunë	ulútië	á luto	lutúla	lutuina	lutië
luvu-	lower, brood	luvo	lúvua	luvui	luvúva	luvunë	ulúvië	á luvo	luvúla	luvuina	luvië
mac-	hew (with sword)	macë	máca	**macë, maci-**	macuva	mancë	amácië	á macë	mácala	mácina	macië
maca-	forge	maca	mácëa	maca	macuva	macanë	amácië	á maca	mácala	macaina	macië
mahta-	wield a weapon	mahta	mahtëa	mahta	mahtuva	mahtanë	amahtië	á mahta	mahtala	mahtaina	mahtië
manca-	trade	manca	mancëa	manca	mancuva	mancanë	amancië	á manca	mancala	mancaina	mancië
manwa-	prepare	manwa	manwëa	manwa	manwuva	manwanë	amanwië	á manwa	manwala	manwaina	manwië
mapa-	grasp	mapa	mapëa	mapa	mapuva	mapanë, mampë	amápië	á mapa	mapala	mapaina	mapië
maquet-	ask	maquetë	maquéta	maquetë,	maquetuva	**maquentë**	amaquétië	á maquetë	maquétala	maquétina	maquétië
mar-	abide	mare	mára	mare	**maruva**	marne	amárie	á mara	márala	marma	marie
marta-	it happens (impersonal)	marta	martëa	marta	martuva	martanë	amartië	á marta	martala	martaina	martië

verbal stem	definition	infinitive	present	aoriste	future	past	perfect	imperative	active pp.	passive pp.	gerund
martya-	destine	martya	martyëa	martya	martyuva	martyanë	amártië	á martya	martyala	martyaina	martië
masta-	bake	masta	mastëa	masta	mastuva	mastanë	amastië	á masta	mastala	mastaina	mastië
mat-	eat	mate	máta	mate, mati-	matuva	**mantë**	amátië	á matë	mátala	mátina	matië
mauya-	compel (+dative)	mauya	mauyëa	mauya	mauyuva	mauyanë	amavië	á mauya	mauyala	mauyaina	mauië
mel-	love	melë	méla	melë, meli-	meluva	mellë	emélië	á melë	mélala	melda	melië
menta-	send, cause to go	menta	mentëa	menta	mentuva	mentanë	ementië	á menta	mentala	mentaina	mentië
mer-	desire	merë	méra	**merë, meri-**	meruva	**mernë**	emérië	ámerë	mérala	merna	merië
metya-	put an end to	metya	metyëa	metya	metyuva	metyanë	emétië	á metya	metyala	metyaina	metië
milya-	long for	milya	milyëa	milya	milyuva	milyanë	imilië	á milya	milyala	milyaina	milië
mina-	wish to go somewh.	mina	minea	mina	minuva	minane	imínië	a mina	minala	mmaina	minië
mirilya-	glitter	mirilya	mirilyëa	mirilya	mirilyuva	mirillë	imirlië	á mirilya	mirilyala	mirilyaina	mirilië
mista-	stray about	mista	mistëa	mista	mistuva	mistanë	imistië	á mista	mistala	mistaina	mistië
mitta-	insert	mitta	mittëa	mitta	mittuva	mittanë	imittië	á mitta	mittala	mittaina	mittië

verbal stem	definition	infinitive	present	aoriste	future	past	perfect	imperative	active pp.	passive pp.	gerund
mittanya- (+allatif)	lead	mittanya	mittanyëa	mittanya	mittanyuva	mittanyanë	imittanië	á mittanya	mittanyala	mittanyaina mittanië	mittanië
moia-	be afflicted	moia	moiëa	moia	moiuva	moianë	omoië	á moia	moiala	moinaina	moië
moru-	hide	moro	mórua	morwë	morúva	morunë	omórië	á moro	morúla	moruina	morië
móta-	labour	móta	mótëa	móta	mótuva	mótanë	omótië	á móta	mótala	mótaina	mótië
muru-	slumber	muro	múrua	murwë, murwi-	murúva	murunë	umúrië	á muro	murúla	muruina	murië
ná-	be		ná	ná, nar	nauva	né, nánë, ané-	anaië	ná! ná!			
nac-	bite	nacë	náca	nacë, naci-	nacuva	nancë	anácië	á nacë	nácala	nácina	nacië
naham-	summon	nahamë	naháma	nahamë, nahami-	nahamuva	nahamnë	anáhamië	á hahamë	nahámala	**nahamna**	nahamië
nahom-	summon	nahomë	nahóma	nahomë	nahomuva	nahomnë	anáhomië	á nahomë	nahómala	**nahomna**	nahomië
nahta-	slay	nahta	nahtëa	nahta	nahtuva	nahtanë	anahtië	á nahta	nahtala	**nahtana,** nahtaina	nahtië
naina-	lament	naina	nainëa	naina	nainuva	nainanë	anánië	á naina	nainala	nainaina	nainië
nainaina-	lament	nainaina	nainainëa	nainaina	nainainuva	nainainë	anainainië	á nainaina	nainainala	nainainaina nainainië	nainainië
naitya-	put shame, abuse	naitya	naityëa	naitya	naituva	naityanë	anaitië	á naitya	naityala	naityaina	naitië

verbal stem	definition	infinitive	present	aoriste	future	past	perfect	imperative	active pp.	passive pp.	gerund
nam-	judge	namë	náma	**namë, nami-**	namuva	namnë	anámië	ánamë	námala	namna	namië
namba-	hammer	namba	nambëa	namba	nambuva	nambanë	anambië	á namba	nambala	nambaina	nambië
nanda-	harp	nanda	nandëa	nanda	nanduva	nandanë	anandië	á nanda	nandala	nandaina	nandië
narca-	rend	narca	narcëa	narca	narcuva	narcanë	anarcië	á narca	narcala	narcaina	narcië
narta-	kindle	narta	nartëa	narta	nartuva	nartanë	anartië	á narta	nartala	nartaina	nartië
nasta-	prick, sting	nasta	nastëa	nasta	nastuva	nastanë	anastië	á nasta	nestala	nastaina	nastië
nattira-	despise	nattira	nattirëa	nattira	nattiruva	nattiranë	anattirië	á nattirë	nattirala	nattima	nattirië
natyam-	summon	natyamë	natyáma	natyamë, natyami-	natyamuva	natyamnë	anatyamië	á natyamë	natyámala	**natyamna**	natyamië
nauta-	conceive, imagine	nauta	nautëa	nauta	nautuva	nautanë	anautië	á nauta	nautala	nautaina	nautië
nav-	judge	navë	náva	**navë, navi-**	navuva	navë	anávië	á navë	navala	navina	navië
netya-	trim, adorn	netya	netyëa	netya	netyuva	netyanë	enétië	á netya	netyala	netyaina	netië
nicu-	be cold (weather)	nico	nícua	niquë, niqui-	nicúva	nicunë	inícië	á nico	n.cúla	nicuina	nicië
ninquita-	shine (white)	ninquita	ninquitëa	ninquita	ninquituva	ninquitanë	ininquitië	á ninquita	n:nquitala	ninquitaina	ninquitië

verbal stem	definition	infinitive	present	aoriste	future	past	perfect	imperative	active pp.	passive pp.	gerund
ninquitá-	whiten	ninquitá	ninquitëa	ninquitá	ninquituva	ninquitanë	ininquitië	á ninquitá	ninquitala	ninquitaina	ninquitië
nir-	force, press, thrust	nirë	níra	**nirë, niri-**	niruva	**nindë**	inirnië	á nira	nirala	nirna	nirië
nornoro-??	run on, run smoothly	nornoro	nornorëa	nornorë, nornori-	nornoruva	nornoronë	onornorië	á nornoro	nornorola	nornoroina	nornorië
nosta-	beget	nosta	nostëa	nosta	nostuva	nostanë	onostië	á nosta	nostala	nostaina	nostië
not-	reckon	note	nóta	note, noti-	notuva	nontë	onótië	á notë	nótala	**nótina**	notië
nuhta-	stop, not allow to	nuhta	nuhtëa	nuhta	nuhtuva	nuhtanë	unuhtië	á nuhta	nuhtala	nuhtaina	nuhtië
numenda-	set (of the sun)	númenda	númendëa	númenda	númenduva	númendanë	unúmendië	á númenda	númendala	númendaina	númendië
númeta-	Set (of thesun)	númeta	númetëa	númeta	númetuva	númetanë	unúmetië	á númeta	númetala	númetaina	númetië
nurru-	murmur, grumble	nurro	nurrua	nurrui	nurrtuva	nurrunë	unurrië	á nurro	nurrula	nurruina	nurrië
nurta-	hide	nurta	nurtëa	nurta	nurtuva	nurtanë	unurtië	á nurta	nurtala	nurtaina	nurtië
nut-	bind, tie	nutë	núta	**nutë, nuti-**	nutuva	nuntë	unútië	á nutë	nútala	nútina	nutië
núta-	set, sink (Sun or Moon)	núta	nútëa	núta	nútuva	nútanë	unútië	á nuta	nútala	nutaina	nutië
nwalya-	pain, torment	nwalya	nwalyëa	nwalya	nwalyuva	nwalyanë	anwálië	á nwalya	nwalyala	nwalyaina	nwalië

verbal stem	definition	infinitive	present	aoriste	future	past	perfect	imperative	active pp.	passive pp.	gerund
nyar-	tell	nyarë	nyára	**nyárë, nyri-**	nyaruva	nyarnë	anyárië	á nyarë	nyárala	nyarna	nyarië
nyéna-	lament	nyéna	nyénëa	nyéna	nyénuva	nyénanë	enyénië	á nyéna	nyénala	nyénaina	nyénië
ohtacar-	war (make war upon)	ohtacarë	ohtacára	ohtacárë,	ohtacaruva	**ohtacarnë**	ohohtacárië, ohtacárië	á ohtacarë	ohtacárala	ohtacarna	ohtacárië
ol-	grow	olë	óla	olë, oli-	oluva	ollë	ololië, olië	á olë	ólala	olda	olië
óla- + datif	dream (impersonal)	óla	ólëa	óla	óluva	olanë	ólólië, ólië	á óla	ólala	ólaina	ólië
oloiya-	flood	oloiya	oloiyëa	oloiya	oloiyuva	oloiyanë	ólólië	á oloiya	oloiyala	oloyaina	óloië
onot-	count up	onotë	onóta	onotë, onoti-onotuva	onotuva	onontë	onótië	á onotë	orótala	onótina	onotië
onta-	beget, create	onta	ontëa	onta	ontuva	**ónë, ontanë**	onontië, ontië	á onta	ontala	ontaina	ontië
or- + datif	impel (impersonal)	orë	óra	**orë, ori-**	**oruva**	**oranë, ornë**	orórië, órië	á ora	órala	orna	orië
ora-	impel (impersonal)	ora	**órëa**	**ora**	**oruva**	**oranë, ornë**	orórië, órië	a ora	órala	oraina	**orië**
orta-	rise, raise	orta	ortëa	orta	ortuva	**ortanë**	orortië, ortië	á orta	ortala	ortaina	ortie
pal-	beat	palë	pála	palë, pali-	paluva	pallë	apálië	á pala	palala	palda	palië
palap-	beat	palapë	palapa	palapë, palapi-	palapuva	palampë	apálapië	á palapa	palapala	palápina	palapië

verbal stem	definition	infinitive	present	aoriste	future	past	perfect	imperative	active pp.	passive pp.	gerund
palpa-	beat	palpa	palpëa	palpa	palpuva	palpanë	apalpië	á palpa	palpala	palpaina	palpië
palu-	open wide	palo	pálua	palwë, palwi-	palúva	palunë	apálië	á palo	palúla	paluina	palië
palya-	spread, open wide	palya	palyëa	palya	palyuva	palyanë	apálië	á palya	palyala	palyaina	palië
panta-	unfurl, open	panta	pantëa	panta	pantuva	pantanë	apantië	á panta	pantala	pantaina	pantië
panya-	Fix, set	panya	panyëa	panya	panyuva	panyanë	apánië	á panya	panyala	panyaina	panië
papa-	tremble	papa	papëa	papa	papuva	papanë, pampë	apapië	á papa	papala	papaina	papië
pel-	go round, return	pelë	péla	pelë, peli-	peluva	pellë	epelië	á pelë	pélala	pelda	pelië
pelecta-	hew	pelecta	pelectëa	pelecta	pelectuva	pelectanë	epélectië	á pelecta	pelectala	pelectaina	pelectië
pelehta-	hew	pelehta	pelehtëa	pelehta	pelehtuva	pelehtanë	epélehtië	á pelehta	pelehtala	pelehtaina	pelehtië
penga-	pout	penga	pengëa	penga	penguva	penganë	epengië	á penga	pengala	pengaina	pengië
perya-	divide in middle	perya	peryëa	perya	peryuva	peryanë	epérië	á perya	peryala	péryaina	perië
pet-	knock, strike	petë	péta	petë, peti-	petuva	**pentë**	epetië	á petë	pétala	pétaina	petië
pica-	lessen	pica	picëa	pica	picuva	picanë	ipícië	á pica	**pícala**	picaina	picië

verbal stem	definition	infinitive	present	aoriste	future	past	perfect	imperative	active pp.	passive pp.	gerund
pir-	spin, turn	pirë	píra	pirë, piri-	piruva	pirnë	ipirië	á pirë	pirala	piraina	pirië
piuta-	spit	piuta	piutëa	piuta	piutuva	piutanë	ipiutië	á piuta	piutala	piutaina	piutië
poita-	clean	poita	poitëa	poita	poituva	**poinë**	opoitië	á poita	poitala	poitaina	poitië
pol-	be able to (physic.)	polë	póla	**polë, poli-**	poluva	pollë	opólië	á polë	pólala	polda	polië
pusta-	stop	pusta	pustëa	pusta	pustuva	pustanë	upustië	á pusta	pustala	pustaina	pustië
qual-	die with suffering	qualë	quála	qualë, quali-	qualuva	quallë	aquálië	á qualë	qualala	qualaina	qualië
qualta-	kill, murder	qualta	qualtëa	qualta	qualtuva	qualtanë	aqualtië	á qualta	qcaltala	qualtaina	qualtië
quat-	fill	quatë	quáta	quatë, quati-	**quantuva**	quantë	aquátië	á quatë	quátala	quátina,	quatië
quel-	fail	quelë	quéla	quelë, queli-	**queluva**	quellë	equélië	á quelë	quelala	quelda	quelië
quer-	turn	querë	quéra	querë, queri-	queruva	quendë	equerië	á querië	querala	**querna**	querië
quet-	say	quetë	quéta	**quetë, queti-**	quetuva	**quentë**	equétië	á quetë	quétala	quétina	quetië
quir-	stir, make spin	quirë	quíra	quirë, quiri-	quiruva	**quindë**	iquitië	á quirë	quirala	quírna	quitië
quoro-??	choke, suffocate	quoro	quorëa	quorë, quori-	quoruva	quoronë	oquoronië	á quoro	quórola	quoroina	quorië

verbal stem	definition	infinitive	present	aoriste	future	past	perfect	imperative	active pp.	passive pp.	gerund
rac-	break	race	ráca	race, raci-	racuva	rancë	arácië	á racë	rácala	**rácina**	racië
racta-	strech out, reach	racta	ractëa	racta	ractuva	ractanë	aractië	á racta	ractala	ractaina	ractië
rahta-	strech out, reach	rahta	rahtëa	rahta	rahtuva	rahtanë	arahtië	á rahta	rahtala	rahtaina	rahtië
raita-/1	make network or lace	raita	raitëa	raita	raituva	raitanë	araitië	á raita	raitala	raitaina	raitië
raita-/2	catch in a net	raita	raitëa	raita	raituva	raitanë	araitië	á raita	raitala	raitaina	raitië
rama-	shout	rama	rámëa	rama	ramuva	ramanë	arámië	árama	rámala	ramaina	ramië
ranya-	stray	ranya	ranyëa	ranya	ranyuva	rannë	arónië	á ranya	ranyala	ranyaina	ranië
rauta-	hunt	rauta	rautëa	rauta	rautuva	rautanë	arautië	á rauta	rautala	rautaina	rautië
rëa-	make network or lace	rëa		rëa		rengë		rëa!			
rem-	snare	remë	réma	**remë, remi-**	remuva	remnë	erémië	á remë	remala	remna	remië
remba-	entrap (in a net)	remba	rembëa	remba	rembuva	rembanë	erembië	á remba	rembala	rembaina	rembië
rer-	sow	rerë	réra	**rerë, reri-**	reruva	**rendë**	erérië	á rerë	rérala	rerna	rerië
ric-	twist	ricë	rica	ricë, rici-	ricuva	rince	**iricië**	á ricë	ricala	ricïna	ricië

verbal stem	definition	infinitive	present	aoriste	future	past	perfect	imperative	active pp.	passive pp.	gerund
rihta-	jerk	rihta	rihtĕa	rihta	rihtuva	rihtanĕ	irihtiĕ	á rihta	rihtala	rihtaina	rihtiĕ
rista-	cut	rista	ristĕa	rista	rista	ristuva	ristanĕ	iristiĕ	á rista	ristala	ristaina	ristiĕ
roita-	hunt (pursue)	roita	roitĕa	roita	roituva	roitanĕ	oroitiĕ	á roita	roitala	roitaina	roitiĕ
ruc-	fear (+ablative)	rucĕ	rúca	**rucĕ, ruci-**	rucuva	runcĕ	urúciĕ	á rucĕ	rúcala	rúcina	ruciĕ
ruc-	fly (take refuge)	rucĕ	rúca	**rucĕ, ruci-**	rucuva	runcĕ	urúciĕ	á rucĕ	rúcala	rúcina	ruciĕ
ruhta-	terrify	ruhta	ruhtĕa	ruhta	ruhtuva	ruhtanĕ	uruhtiĕ	á ruhta	ruⁱhta	ruhtaina	ruhtiĕ
rúma-	heave (intransitive, of heavy things)	rúma	rúmĕa	rúma	rúmuva	rúmanĕ	urúmiĕ	á rúma	**rúmala**	rúmaina	rúmiĕ
rúna-	free	rúna	rúnĕa	rúna	rúnuva	rúnanĕ	urúniĕ	á rúna	rúnala	rúnaina	rⁱniĕ
ruxa-	crumble	ruxa	rúxĕa	ruxa	ruxuva	ruxanĕ	urúxiĕ	á ruxa	**ruxala**	ruxaina	ruxiĕ
saca- /1	pursue, look for	saca	sacĕa	saca	sacuva	**sácĕ**	asáciĕ	á saca	sacala	sacaina	saciĕ
saca- /2	draw, pull	saca	sacĕa	saca	sacuva	**sácĕ**	asáciĕ	á saca	sacala	sacaina	saciĕ
sahta-	induce	sahta	sahtĕa	sahta	sahtuva	sahtanĕ	asahtiĕ	á sahta	sahtala	sahtaina	**sahtiĕ**
saita-	teach	saita	saitĕa	saita	saituva	saitanĕ	asaitiĕ	á saita	saitala	saitaina	saitiĕ

verbal stem	definition	infinitive	present	aoriste	future	past	perfect	imperative	active pp.	passive pp.	gerund
salpa-	lick up, sup, sip	salpa	salpëa	salpa	salpuva	salpanë	asalpië	á salpa	salpala	salpaina	salpië
sana-	think, reflect	sana	sanëa	sana	sanuva	sananë	asánië	á sana	sánala	sanaina	sanië
sat-	set aside	satë	sáta	satë, sati-	satuva	santë	asatië	á satë	sátala	sátina	satië
sen-	let loose, free, let go	senë	séna	senë, sem-	senuva	senne	esénië	a senë	sénala	senna	semë
ser-	rest	serë	séra	serë, sen-	seruva	sendë	esérië	á serë	serala	serma	senë
serta-	bind, tie	serta	sertëa	serta	sertuva	sérë	esertië	á serta	sertala	sertaina	sertië
sil-	shine (with white light)	silë	síla	silë, sili-	siluva	sillë	isilië	á silë	silala	silda	silië
sinta-	fade	sinta	sintëa	sinta	sintuva	sintanë	isintië	á sinta	sintala	sintaina	sintië
sir-	flow	sirë	síra	sirë, siri-	siruva	sirnë	isírië	á sirë	sirala	sirna	sirië
sisila-	shine (white) freq.	sisila	sisilëa	sisila	sisiluva	sisilanë	isisilië	á sisila	sisilala	sisilaina	sisilië
suc-	drink	sucë	súca	sucë, suci-	sucuva	suncë	usúcië	á sucë	sucala	súcina	sucië
sulp-	lick	sulpë	sulpa	sulpë, sulpi-	sulpuva	sulppë	usulpië	á sulpë	sulpala	sulpina	sulpië
súya-	breathe	súya	súyëa	súya	súyuva	súnë	usúië	á súya	súyala	súyaina	súië

verbal stem	definition	infinitive	present	aoriste	future	past	perfect	imperative	active pp.	passive pp.	gerund
tac-	fasten	tacë	táca	**tacë, taci-**	tacuva	**tancë**	atácië	á tacë	tácala	tácina	tacië
taita-	prolong	taita	taitëa	taita	taituva	taitanë	atáitië	á taita	taitala	taitaina	taitië
talat-	slip, fall down	talatë	talata	talatë, talati-	talatuva	talatanë	atalatië	á talatë	talatala	talataina	talatië
talta-	collapse, slide down	talta	taltëa	talta	taltuva	taltanë	ataltië	á talta	**taltala**	taltaina	taltië
tam-	tap	tamë	táma	**tamë, tami-**	tamuva	**tamnë**	atámië	á tamë	tamala	tamna	tamië
tamba-	knock	tamba	tambëa	tamba	tambuva	tambanë	atambië	á tamba	tambala	tambaina	tambië
tan-	do, fashion	tanë	tána	tanë, tani-	tanuva	tamnë	atanië	á tanë	tánala	tanna	tanië
tana-	indicate, show	tana	tanëa	tana	tanuva	tananë	atánië	á tana	tanala	tanaina	tanië
tanta-	harp	tanta	tantëa	tanta	tantuva	tantanë	atantië	á tanta	tantala	tantaina	tantië
tap-	stop, block	tape	tápa	**tapë, tapi-**	tapuva	**tampë**	atápië	á tape	tapala	tápina	tapie
tatya-	double	tatya	tatyëa	tatya	tatyuva	tatyanë	atátië	á tatya	tatyalá	tatyaina	tatië
tëa-	indicate		tëa			**tengë**					
tec-	write	tecë	téca	**tecë, teci-**	tecuva	tencë	etécië	á tecë	tecala	técina	tecië

verbal stem	definition	infinitive	present	aoriste	future	past	perfect	imperative	active pp.	passive pp.	gerund
telconta-	stride	telconta	telcontëa	telconta	telcontuva	telcontanë	etelcontië	á telconta	telcontala	telcontaina	telcontië
telë-	end (intransitive)	telë	téla	**telë, teli-**	teluva	telenë	etélië	á telë	telela	télina	telië
telta-	overshadow	telta	teltëa	telta	teltuva	teltanë	eteltië	á telta	teltala	teltaina	teltië
telya-	conclude (trans.)	telya	telyëa	telya	telyuva	telyanë	etélië	á telya	telyala	telyaina	telië
ten-	hear	tenë	téna	tenë, teni-	tenuva	tennë	eténië	á tenë	tenala	tenna	tenië
terhat-	break apart	terhatë	terháta	terhatë, terhati-	terhatuva	**terhantë**	eterhátië	á terhatë	terhátala	terhátina	terhátië
tevë-	hate	tevë	téva	**tevë, tevi-**	tevuva	tévenë	etévië	á tevë	tevala	tévina	tevië
tihta-	blink (peer)	tihta	tihtëa	tihta	tihtuva	tihtanë	itihtië	á tihta	**tihtala**	tihtaina	tihtië
tin-	glint	tinë	tína	**tinë, tini-**	tinuva	tinnë	itinië	á tinë	tinala	tinna	tinië
tinga-	twang, make a twang	tinga	tingëa	tinga	tinguva	tinguva	itingië	á tinga	tingala	tingaina	tingië
tinta-	twinkle	tinta	tintëa	tinta	tintuva	tintanë	itintië	á tinta	tintala	tintaina	tintië
tintila-	kindel	tintila	tintilëa	**tintila**	tintiluva	tintilanë	itintilië	á tintila	tintila	tintilaina	tintilië
tintina-	sparkle	tintina	tintinëa	tintina	tintinuva	tintinanë	itintinië	á tintina	tintinala	tintinaina	tintinië

verbal stem	definition	infinitive	present	aoriste	future	past	perfect	imperative	active pp.	passive pp.	gerund
tir-	watch	tire	tíra	**tírë, tíri-**	**tíruva**	tirnë	itírië	**tíra**, á tíra	tirala	tirna	tírië
tiuta-	comfort	tiuta	tiutëa	tiuta	tiutuva	tiutanë	utiutië	á tiuta	tiutala	tiutaina	tiutië
tiuya-	swell	tiuya	tiuyëa	tiuya	tiuyuva	tiunë	utúië	á tiuya	tiuyala	tiuyaina	tiuië?
top-	cover	topë	tópa	**topë, topi-**	topuva	**tompë**	otópië	á topë	tópala	tópina	topië
tópa-	roof	tópa	tópëa	tópa	tópuva	tópanë	otópië	á tópa	tópala	tópaina	tópaië
tuc-	draw	tucë	túca	**tucë, tuci-**	tucuva	tuncë	utúcië	á tuce	tucala	túcina	tucië
tuia-	sprout	tuia	tuiëa	tuia	tuiuva	tuianë	utúië	á tuia	tuiala	tuiaina	tuië
tul-	come	tulë	túla	**tulë, tuli-**	tuluva	**tulle**	**utúlië**	á tulë	tulala	tulda	tulië
tulca-	establish, fix	tulca	tulcëa	tulca	tulcuva	tulcanë	utalcië	á tulca	tulca	tulcaina	tulcië
tulta-	fetch, summon	tulta	tultëa	tulta	tultuva	tultanë	utultië	á tulta	tultala	tultaina	tultië
tulu-	bring, bear, come	tulo	túlua	tulwë, tulwi-	tulúva	tulunë	utúlië	á tulo	tulúla	tuluina	tulië
tulya- + allatif	lead	tulya	tulyëa	tulya	tulyuva	tulyanë	utilië	á tulya	tulyala	tulyaina	tulië
tup-	cover	tupë	túpa	tupë, tupi-	tupuva	tumpë	utúpië	á tupë	tupala	túpina	tupië

verbal stem	definition	infinitive	present	aoriste	future	past	perfect	imperative	active pp.	passive pp.	gerund
tur-	govern	turë	túra	turë, turi-	turuva	turnë	utúrië	á turë	turala	turna	turië
turu-	kindle	turo	túrua	turwë, turwi-	turúva	turuë	utúrië	á turo	turúla	turuina	turië
tuv-	find	tuvë	túva	tuvë, tuvi-	tuvuva	túvë	**utúvië**	á tuvë	túvala	túvina	tuvië
tuvu-	receive	tuvo	túvua	tuvui	tuvúva	tuvunë	utúvië	á tuvo	tuvúla	tuvuina	tuvië
tyal-	play	tyalë	tyála	**tyalë, tyali-**	tyaluva	tyallë	atyálië	á tyalë	tyálala	tyalda	tyalië
tyar-	cause	tyarë	tyára	tyarë, tyari-	tyaruva	tyarnë	atyárië	á tyarë	tyárala	tyárina	tyarië
tyav-	taste	tyavë	tyáva	**tyavë, tyavi-**	tyavuva	tyávë	atyávië	á tyavë	tyávala	tyávina	tyavië
tyel-	end, cease	tyelë	tyéla	tyelë, tyeli-	tyeluva	tyellë	etyélië	á tyelë	tyélala	tyelda	tyelië
tyulta-	stand up	tyulta	tyultëa	tyulta	tyultuva	tyultanë	utyultië	á tyulta	tyultala	tyultaina	tyultië
úcar-	sin	úcarë	úcára	**úcarë, úcari-**	úcaruva	úcarnë	úcarië, *úacarië	á úcarë	úcarala	úcarna, úcarina	úcarië
ulya-	pour (intransitive)	ulya	úlëa	ulya	ulyuva	**ullë**	ulúlië, ulië	á ulya	ulyala	ulyaina	ulië
ulya-	pour (transitive)	ulya	úlëa	ulya	ulyuva	**ulyanë,**	ulúlië, ulië	á ulya	ulyala	ulyaina	ulië
um-	not be, not do	umë	umëa	**umë, umi-**	**úva**	**úmë**	uhúmië, húmië	á umë	umela	umna	umië

verbal stem	definition	infinitive	present	aoriste	future	past	perfect	imperative	active pp.	passive pp.	gerund
uma-	swarm, stir	uma	uměa	uma	umuva	umaně	uhúmië	á uma	umala	umaina	umië
unca-	hollow out	unca	uncěa	unca	uncuva	uncaně	uhuncië, hunciě	á unca	uncala	uncaina	uncië
untúpa-	cover, down-roof	untúpa	untúpěa	untúpa	untúpuva	untúpaně	untúpië	á untúpa	untúpala	untúpaina	untúpië
urta-	burn (transitive)	urta	urtěa	urta	urtuva	urtaně	urtië, ururtië, urrurtië	á urta	urtala	urtaina	urtië
urya-	burn (intransitive)	urya	uryěa	urya	uryuva	uryaně	urúrië, úrië	á urya	uryala	uryaina	urië
us-	escape	usě	úsa	usě, usi-	usuva	ussě, úsě	usúsië, úsië	á usě	úsala	úsina	usië
usta-	burn (transitive)	usta	ustěa	usta	ustuva	ustaně	usústië, ustië	á usta	ustala	ustaina	ustië
vahta-	stain	vahta	vahtěa	vahta	vahtuva	vahtaně	avahtië, vahtië	á vahta	vahtala	vahtaina	vahtië
vaita-	clothe	vaita	vaitěa	vaita	vaituva	vaitaně	avaitië, vaitië	á vaita	vaitala	vaitaina	vaitië
vala-	rule (divine power)	vála	valěa	valě, vali-	valuva	valaně	aválië, válië	á vala	válala	valaina	valië
vanta-	walk	vanta	vantěa	vanta	vantuva	vantaně	avantië, vantië	á vanta	vantala	vantaina	vantië
vanya-	depart	vanya	vanyěa	vanya	vanyuva	vanně	avánië, vánië	á vanya	vanyala	vanyaina	vanië
váquet-	refuse, say no	váquetě	váquěta	váquetě, váqueti-	váquetuva	váquentě	aváquétië, vaquetië	á váquetě	váquétala	váquetina	váquetië

verbal stem	definition	infinitive	present	aoriste	future	past	perfect	imperative	active pp.	passive pp.	gerund
varya-	protect	varya	varyëa	varya	varyuva	varyanë	avárië, várië	á varya	varyala	varma	varie
vasarya-	veil	vasarya	vasaryëa	vasarya	vasaryuva	vasaryanë	avásarië, vásarië	á vasarya	vasaryala	vasaryaina	vasarië
vél-	see	velë	véla	velë, veli-	véluva	vélanë	evélië, vélië	á véla	vélala	vélda	vélië
verya-	dare	verya	veryëa	verya	veryuva	veryanë	evérië, vérië	á verya	veryala	veryaina	verië
vesta-	wed	vesta	vestëa	vesta	vestuva	vestanë	evestië, vestië	á vesta	vestala	vestaina	vestië
veuya-	follow, serve	veuya	veuyëa	veuya	veuyuva	veuyanë	evéwië	á veuya	veuyala	veyuina	vevië
vil-	fly	vile	vila	**vilë, vili-**	viluva	**villë**	ivilië, vilië	á vilë	vilala	vilda	vilië
vinda-	fade	vinda	vindëa	vinda	vinduva	**vindanë**	ivindië, vindië	á vinda	vindala	vindaina	vindië
vinta-	fade	vinta	vintëa	vinta	vintuva	**vinté, vintanë**	ivintië, vintië	á vinta	vintala	vintaina	vintië
waita-	clothe	waita	waitëa	waita	waituva	waitanë	awaitië	á waita	waitala	waitaina	waitië
wil-	fly	wilë	wïla	**wilë, wïli-**	wiluva	**willë**	iwïlië, wïlië	á wilë	wilala	wilda	wïlië
winta-	scatter, blow about	winta	wintëa	winta	wintuva	wintanë	iwintië, wintië	á winta	wintala	wintaina	wintië
yal-	summon	yalë	yála	yalë, yali-	yaluva	yallë	ayálië, yálië	á yalë	yálala	yalda	yalië

verbal stem	definition	infinitive	present	aoriste	future	past	perfect	imperative	active pp.	passive pp.	gerund
yanga-	yawn	yanga	yangëa	yanga	yanguva	yanganë	ayangië, yangië	á yanga	yangala	yangaina	yangië
yarra-	growl, snarl	yarra	yarrëa	yarra	yarruva	yarranë	ayarrië	á yarra	yarrala	yarraina	yarrië
yav-	bear fruit	yavë	yáva	**yavë, yavi-**	yavuva	yávë	ayávië	áyavë	yávala	yávina	yavië
yelta-	loathe, abhor	yelta	yeltëa	yelta	yeltuva	yeltanë	eyeltië	á yelta	yeltala	yeltaina	yeltië
yerya-	get old	yerya	yeryëa	yerya	yeryuva	yernë	eyérië	á yerya	yeryala	yeryaina	yerië
yesta-	desire	yesta	yestëa	yesta	yestuva	yestanë	ehyestië	á yesta	yestala	yestaina	yestië
yéta-	look at	yéta	yétëa	yéta	yétuva	yétanë	eyétië	á yéta	yétala	yétaina	yétië
yuhta-	use	yuhta	yuhtëa	yuhta	yuhtuva	yuhtanë	uyuhtië	á yuhta	yuhtala	yuhtaina	yuhtië
yulu-	bear	yulo	yúlua	yulwë, yulwi-	yuliúva	yulunë	ayúlië	á yulo	yulúla	yuluina	yulië
yur-	run	yurë	yúra	**yurë, yuri-**	yuruva	yurnë	uyúrië	á yurë	yurala	yurna	yurië

English-Quenya

definition	verbal stem	infinitive	present	aoriste	future	past	perfect	imperative	active pp.	passive pp.	gerund
come back, return	**entul-**	entulë	entúla	entulë, entuli-	entuluva	entullë	entúlië	á entulë	entulala	entulda	entulië
free, let loose, let go	**sen-**	senë	séna	senë, sem-	senuva	semne	esénië	á senë	sénala	senna	semë
abandon, put aside	**hehta-**	hehta	hehtëa	hehta	hehtuva	**hehtanë**	ehehtië	á hehta	hehtala	hehtaina	hehtië
abhor, feel disgust at	**feuya-**	feuya	feuyëa	feuya	feuyuva	feuyanë	efëwië	á feuya	feuyala	feuyaina	feuië
abhor, loathe	**yelta-**	yelta	yeltëa	yelta	yeltuva	yeltanë	eyeltië	á yelta	yeltala	yeltaina	yeltië
abide	**mar-**	mare	mára	mare	**maruva**	marne	amárie	á mara	márala	marna	marie
abide by, stick, adhere	**himya-**	himya	himyëa	himya	himyuva	himyanë	ihímië	á himya	himyala	himyaina	himië
abuse, put shame	**naitya-**	naitya	naityëa	naitya	naituva	naityanë	anaitië	á naitya	naityala	naityaina	naitië
accommodate	**camta-**	camta	camtëa	camta	camtuva	camtanë	acámië	á camta	camtala	camtaina	camtië
adhere, abide by, stick	**himya-**	himya	himyëa	himya	himyuva	himyanë	ihímië	á himya	himyala	himyaina	himië
adorn, trim	**netya-**	netya	netyëa	netya	netyuva	netyanë	enétië	á netya	netyala	netyaina	netië
affect, concern	**ap-**	apë	ápa	apë, api-	apuva	ampë	ápië, apápië	á apë	ápala	ápina	apië
allow	**lav-**	lave	láva	lavë, lavi-	lavuva	**lávë**	alávië	á lavë	lávala	lávina	lavië

Presented by http://www.ambar-eldaron.com

definition	verbal stem	infinitive	present	aoriste	future	past	perfect	imperative	active pp.	passive pp.	gerund
ask	**maquet-**	maquetë	maquéta	maquetë,	maquetuva	**maquentë**	amaquétië	á maquetë	maquétala	maquétina	maquétië
bake	**masta-**	masta	mastëa	masta	mastuva	mastanë	amastië	á masta	mastala	mastaina	mastië
ban, drive out	*etementa-	etementa	etementëa	etementa	etementuva	etementanë	etementië, etementië	á etementa	etementala	etementaina	etementië
be	**ná-**		**ná**	**ná, nar**	**nauva**	**né, nánë, ané-**	**anaië**	na! ná!			
be able to (physic.)	pol-	polë	póla	**polë, poli-**	poluva	pollë	opólië	á polë	pólala	polda	polië
be afflicted	**moia-**	moia	moiëa	moia	moiuva	moianë	omoië	á moia	moiala	moinaina	moië
be cold (weather)	nicu-	nico	nícua	niquë, niqui-	nicúva	nicunë	imícië	á nico	nicúla	nicuina	nicië
be compelled to do something, have an	horya-	horya	horyëa	horya	horyuva	hornë	ohórië	á horya	horyala	horyaina	horië
be free to do, can	**lerta-**	lerta	lertëa	**lerta**	lertuva	lertanë	elertië	á lerta	lertala	lertaina	lertië
be, exist	ëa	ëa		ëa		**engë**		ëa!			
bear	**col-**	colë	cóla	colë, coli-	coluva	collë	ocólië	á colë	cólala	**colla**	colië
bear	**yulu-**	yulo	yúlua	yulwë, yulwi-, yuliü-	yulüva	yulunë	ayúlië	á yulo	yulúla	yuluina	yulië
bear fruit	**yav-**	yavë	yáva	**yavë, yavi-**	yavuva	yávë	ayávië	á yavë	yávala	yávina	yavië

Presented by http://www.ambar-eldaron.com

definition	verbal stem	infinitive	present	aoriste	future	past	perfect	imperative	active pp.	passive pp.	gerund
beat	**pal-**	palë	pála	palë, pali-	paluva	pallë	apálië	á pala	palala	palda	palië
beat	**palap-**	palapë	palapa	palapë, palapi-	palapuva	palampë	apálapië	á palapa	palapala	palápina	palapië
beat	**palpa-**	palpa	palpëa	palpa	palpuva	palpanë	apalpië	á palpa	palpala	palpaina	palpië
beget	**nosta-**	nosta	nostëa	nosta	nostuva	nostanë	onostië	á nosta	nostala	nostaina	nostië
beget, create	onta-	onta	ontëa	onta	ontuva	**ónë, ontanë**	onontië, ontië	á onta	ontala	ontaina	ontië
bend (intr.)	**cúna-**	cúna	cúnëa	cúna	cúnuva	cúnanë	ucúnië	á cúna	cúnala	cúnaina	cunië
bind, deprive of liberty	***avalerya-**	avalerya	avaleryëa	avalerya	avaleryuva	avalemë	ávalérië	á avalerya	avaleryala	avaleryaina	avalerië
bind, tie	**nut-**	nutë	núta	**nutë, nuti-**	nutuva	nuntë	umútië	á nutë	nútala	nútina	nutië
bind, tie	**serta-**	serta	sertëa	serta	sertuva	**sérë**	esertië	á serta	sertala	sertaina	sertië
bite	**nac-**	nacë	náca	nacë, naci-	nacuva	nancë	anácië	á nacë	nácala	nácina	nacië
bless	**laita-**	laita	laitëa	laita	**laituva**	laitanë	alaitië	**á laita**	laitala	laitaina	laitië
bless, dread	**aista-**	aista	aistëa	aista	aistuva	aistanë	ahaistië	á aista	aistala	**aistana**	aistië
blink (peer)	**tihta-**	tihta	tihtëa	tihta	tihtuva	tihtanë	itihtië	á tihta	**tihtala**	tihtaina	tihtië

definition	verbal stem	infinitive	present	aoriste	future	past	perfect	imperative	active pp.	passive pp.	gerund
block, stop	**tap-**	tape	tápa	**tapë, tapi-**	tapuva	**tampë**	atápië	á tape	tapala	tápina	tapie
Bloom	**losta-**	losta	lostëa	losta	lostuva	lostanë	olostië	á losta	lostala	lostaina	lostië
blow about, scatter	**winta-**	winta	wintëa	winta	wintuva	wintanë	iwintië, wintië	á winta	wintala	wintaina	wintië
blow, fly or stream in the wind	**hlapu-**	hlapo	hlápua	hlapui	hlapúva	hlapunë	ahlápië	á hlapo	**hlápula**	hlapuina	hlapië
bow	**luhta-**	luhta	luhtëa	luhta	luhtuva	luhtanë	uluhtië	á luhta	luhtala	luhtaina	luhtië
break	**rac-**	race	ráca	race, raci-	racuva	rancë	arácië	á racë	rácala	**rácina**	racië
break apart	**terhat-**	terhatë	terháta	terhatë, terhati-	terhatuva	**terhantë**	eterhátië	á terhatë	terhátala	terhátina	terhátië
break asunder	**ascat-**	ascatë	ascáta	ascatë, ascati-	ascatuva	**ascantë**	ascátië	á ascatë	ascatala	ascatina	ascatië
break asunder	**hat-**	hatë	háta	hatë, hati-	hatuva	**hantë**	ahátië	á hatë	hátala	hátina	hatië
breathe	**súya-**	súya	súyëa	súya	súyuva	súnë	usúië	á súya	súyala	súyaina	súië
bring, bear, come	**tulu-**	tulo	túlua	tulwë, tulwi-	tulúva	tulunë	utúlië	á tulo	tulúla	tuluina	tulië
brood, lower	**luvu-**	luvo	lúvua	luvui	luvúva	luvunë	ulúvië	á luvo	luvúla	luvuina	luvië
build	**car-**	carë	cára	carë, cari-	caruva	**carnë**	**cárië**, acárië	**á carë**	cárala	**carna, carina**	carië

definition	verbal stem	infinitive	present	aoriste	future	past	perfect	imperative	active pp.	passive pp.	gerund
burn (intransitive)	**urya-**	urya	uryëa	urya	uryuva	uryanë	urúrië, úrië	á urya	uryala	uryaina	urië
burn (transitive)	**urta-**	urta	urtëa	urta	urtuva	urtanë	urtië, ururtië, urturtië	á urta	urtala	urtaina	urtië
burn (transitive)	**usta-**	usta	ustëa	usta	ustuva	ustanë	usústië, ustië	á usta	ustala	ustaina	ustië
can, be free to do	**lerta-**	lerta	lertëa	**lerta**	lertuva	lertanë	elertië	a lerta	lertala	lertaina	lertië
catch in a net	**raita-/2**	raita	raitëa	raita	raituva	raitanë	araitië	á raita	raitala	raitaina	raitië
cause	**tyar-**	tyarë	tyára	tyárë, tyari-	tyaruva	tyarnë	atyárië	á tyarë	tyárala	tyárina	tyarië
cause to go, send	**menta-**	menta	mentëa	menta	mentuva	mentanë	ementië	á menta	mentala	mentaina	mentië
cease, end	**tyel-**	tyelë	tyéla	tyélë, tyeli-	tyeluva	tyellë	etyélië	á tyelë	tyélala	tyelda	tyelië
cease, take rest, stop	**hauta-**	hauta	hautëa	hauta	hautuva	hautanë	ahautië	á hauta	hautala	hautaina	hautië
change	**ahya-**	ahya	ahyëa	ahya	ahyuva	**ahyanë**	aháhië, háhië	á ahya	ahyala	ahyaina	ahië
choke, suffocate	**quoro-??**	quoro	quorëa	quorë, quori-	quoruva	quoronë	oquoronië	á quoro	quórola	quoroina	quorië
choose	***cil-**	cilë	cíla	cilë, cil-	ciluva	cillë	icilië	á cilë	cilala	cilda	cilië
clean	**poita-**	poita	poitëa	poita	poituva	**poinë**	opoitië	á poita	poitala	poitaina	poitië

definition	verbal stem	infinitive	present	aoriste	future	past	perfect	imperative	active pp.	passive pp.	gerund
cleave	**hyar-**	hyarë	hyára	**hyarë, hyari-**	hyaruva	**hyandë**	ahyárië	á hyarë	hyárala	hyarna	hyarië
cleave, divide	*cilta-	cilta	ciltëa	cilta	ciltuva	ciltanë	iciltië	á cilta	ciltala	ciltaina	ciltië
cloak, veil	**fanta-**	fanta	fantëa	fanta	fantuva	fantanë	afantië	á fanta	fantala	fantaina	fantië
close	**avalatya-**	avalatya	avalatyëa	avalatya	avalatyuva	avalatyanë	ávalátië	á avalatya	avalatyala	avalatyaina	avalatië
clothe	**vaita-**	vaita	vaitëa	vaita	vaituva	vaitanë	avaitië, vaitië	á vaita	vaitala	vaitaina	vaitië
clothe	**waita-**	waita	waitëa	waita	waituva	waitanë	awaitië	á waita	waitala	waitaina	waitië
collapse, fall in	**atalta-**	atalta	ataltëa	atalta	ataltuva	**ataltanë**	atáltië	á atalta	ataltala	ataltaina	ataltië
collapse, slide down	**talta-**	talta	taltëa	talta	taltuva	taltanë	ataltië	á talta	**taltala**	taltaina	taltië
collect, gather	**hosta-**	hosta	hostëa	hosta	hostuva	hostanë	ohostië	á hosta	hostala	**hostaina**	hostie
come forth	**ettul-**	ettulë	ettúla	ettulë, ettuli-	ettuluva	ettullë	ettulië	á ettulë	ettulala	ettulaina	ettulië
comfort	**tiuta-**	tiuta	tiutëa	tiuta	tiutuva	tiutanë	utiutië	á tiuta	tiutala	tiutaina	tiutië
command, order	**can-**	canë	cána	canë, cani-	canuva	cannë	acánië	á canë	cánala	canna	canië
compel (+dative)	**mauya-**	mauya	mauyëa	mauya	mauyuva	mauyanë	amavië	á mauya	mauyala	mauyaina	mauië

Presented by http://www.ambar-eldaron.com

definition	verbal stem	infinitive	present	aoriste	future	past	perfect	imperative	active pp.	passive pp.	gerund
conceal, lie	**fur-**	furë	fíra	furë, furi-	furuva	furnë	ufúrië	á furë	furala	furna	furië
conceal, lie	**hur-**	hurë	húra	hurë, huri-	huruva	hurnë	uhúrië	á hurë	hú::rala	hurna	hurië
conceive, screen from the light	**halya-**	halya	halyëa	halya	halyuva	halyanë	ahálië	á halya	halyala	halyaina	halië
conceive, imagine	**nauta-**	nauta	nautëa	nauta	nautuva	nautanë	anautië	á nauta	nautala	nautaina	nautië
concern, affect	**ap-**	apë	ápa	**apë, api-**	apuva	ampë	ápië, apápië	á apë	ápala	ápina	apië
conclude (trans.)	**telya-**	telya	telyëa	telya	telyuva	telyanë	etélië	á telya	telyala	telyaina	telië
continually grow	**alála-**	alála	alálëa	alála	aláluva	alálanë	álië, alálië	á alála	alálala	alálaina	alálië
come	**tul-**	tulë	túla	**tulë, tuli-**	tuluva	**tulle**	**utúlië**	á tulë	tulala	tulda	tulië
count up	**onot-**	onotë	onóta	onotë, onoti-onotuva	onotuva	onotë	onótië	á onotë	onótala	onótina	onotië
cover	**top-**	topë	tópa	**topë, topi-**	topuva	**tompë**	otópië	á topë	tópala	tópina	topië
cover	**tup-**	tupë	túpa	tupë, tupi-	tupuva	tumpë	utúpië	á tupë	tupala	túpina	tupië
cover, down-roof	**untúpa-**	untúpa	untúpëa	untúpa	untúpuva	untúpanë	untúpië	á untúpa	untúpala	untúpaina	untúpië
create, beget	**onta-**	onta	ontëa	onta	ontuva	**ónë, ontanë**	onontië, ontië	á onta	ontala	ontaina	ontië

Presented by http://www.ambar-eldaron.com

definition	verbal stem	infinitive	present	aoriste	future	past	perfect	imperative	active pp.	passive pp.	gerund
crumble	**ruxa-**	ruxa	rúxëa	ruxa	ruxuva	ruxanë	urúxië	á ruxa	**ruxala**	ruxaina	ruxië
cut	**rista-**	rista	ristëa	rista	ristuva	ristanë	iristië	á rista	ristala	ristaina	ristië
cut off	**hóciri-**	hócirë	**hócira**	**hócirë**	hóciruva	**hócirnë**	ohócirië	á hócirë	hócirila	hócirina	hócirië
dance	**lilta-**	lilta	liltëa	lilta	liltuva	liltanë	ililtië	á lilta	liltala	liltaina	liltië
dangle, hang	**linga-**	linga	lingëa	linga	linguva	linganë	ilingië	á linga	lingala	lingaina	lingië
dare	**verya-**	verya	veryëa	verya	veryuva	veryanë	evérië, vérië	á verya	veryala	veryaina	verië
deliver	**etrúna-**	eterúna	aterúnëa	eterúna	eterúnuva	eterúnanë	etrúnië	á eterúna	eterúnala	eterúnaina	eterúnië
deliver	**eterúna-**	eterúna	aterúnëa	eterúna	eterúnuva	eterúnanë	eterúnië	á eterúna	eterúnala	eterúnaina	eterúnië
deliver (save)	**etelehta-**	etelehta	etelehtëa	etelehta	etelehtuva	etelehtanë	etelehtië	á etelehta	etelehtala	etelehtaina	etelehtië
deny	**lala-**	lala	lálëa	lala	laluva	lalanë, lallë	aldalië,	á lala	lalala	lalaina	lalië
deny	**laquet-**	laquetë	laqueta	laquetë, laqueti-	laquetuva	laquentë	alaquetië	á laquetë	laquétala	laquétina	laquetië
depart	**vanya-**	vanya	vanyëa	vanya	vanyuva	**vannë**	avánië, vánië	á vanya	vanyala	vanyaina	vanië
deprive of liberty, bind	***avalerya-**	avalerya	avaleryëa	avalerya	avaleryuva	avalernë	ávalérië	á avalerya	avaleryala	avaleryaina	avalerië

definition	verbal stem	infinitive	present	aoriste	future	past	perfect	imperative	active pp.	passive pp.	gerund
desire	**mer-**	merë	méra	**merë, meri-**	meruva	**mernë**	emérië	á merë	mérala	merna	merië
desire	**yesta-**	yesta	yestëa	yesta	yestuva	yestanë	ehyestië	á yesta	yestala	yestaina	yestië
despise	**nattira-**	nattira	nattirëa	nattira	nattiruva	nattiranë	anattirië	á nattirë	nattirala	nattirna	nattirië
destine	**martya-**	martya	martyëa	martya	martyuva	martyanë	amártië	á martya	martyala	martyaina	martië
die with suffering	qual-	qualë	quála	qualë, quali-	qualuva	quallë	aquálië	á qualë	qualala	qualaina	qualië
die, expire	**effir-**	effirë	effira	effirë	effiruva	effirnë	effirië	á effirë	effirala	effirna	**effirië**
die, fade	**fir-**	firë	fira	**firë, firi-**	firuva	firnë	ifirië, **firië**	á firë	firala	firna	firië
distribute in even portions	**etsat-**	etsatë	etsáta	etsatë, etsati-	etsatuva	etsantë	etsatië	á etsatë	estsátala	etsatina	etsatië
divide in middle	**perya-**	perya	peryëa	perya	peryuva	peryanë	epérië	á perya	peryala	péryaina	perië
divide, cleave	*cilta-	cilta	ciltëa	cilta	ciltuva	ciltanë	iciltië	á cilta	ciltala	ciltaina	ciltië
do, fashion	**tan-**	tanë	tána	tanë, tani-	tanuva	tamë	atanië	á tanë	tánala	tanna	tanië
double	**tatya-**	tatya	tatyëa	tatya	tatyuva	tatyanë	atátië	á tatya	tatyala	tatyaina	tatië
down-roof, cover	**untúpa-**	untúpa	untúpëa	untúpa	untúpuva	untúpanë	untúpië	á untúpa	untúpala	untúpaina	untúpië

definition	verbal stem	infinitive	present	aoriste	future	past	perfect	imperative	active pp.	passive pp.	gerund
draw	tuc-	tucë	túca	tucë, tuci-	tucuva	tuncë	utúcië	á tuce	tucala	túcina	tucië
draw water	calpa-	calpa	calpëa	calpa	calpuva	calpanë	acalpië	á calpa	calpala	calpaina	calpië
draw, pull	saca-/2	saca	sacëa	saca	sacuva	sácë	asácië	á saca	sacala	sacaina	sacië
dread	alta-	alta	altëa	alta	altuva	altanë	áltië, aláltië	á alta	altala	altaina	altië
dread, bless	aista-	aista	aistëa	aista	aistuva	aistanë	ahaistië	á aista	aistala	aistana	aistië
dream (impersonal)	óla- + datif	óla	ólëa	óla	óluva	olanë	ólólië, ólië	á óla	ólala	ólaina	ólië
drink	suc-	sucë	súca	sucë, suci-	sucuva	suncë	usúcië	á sucë	sucala	súcina	sucië
drive out, ban	*etementa-	etementa	etementëa	etementa	etementuva	etementanë	etementië, etementië	á etementa	etementala	etementaina	etementië
eat	mat-	mate	máta	mate, mati-	matuva	mantë	amátië	á matë	mátala	mátina	matië
emit light	faina-	faina	fainëa	faina	fainuva	fainanë	afainië	á faina	fainala	fainaina	fainië
emit light	farya-	farya	faryëa	farya	faryuva	farnë	afárië	á farya	faryala	faryaina,	farië
enchant	luhta-	luhta	luhtëa	luhta	luhtuva	luhtanë	uluhtië	á luhta	luhtala	luhtaina	luhtië
enclose, bound	lanya-	lanya	lanyëa	lanya	lanyuva	lanyanë	alánië	á lanya	lanyala	lanyaina	lanië

definition	verbal stem	infinitive	present	aoriste	future	past	perfect	imperative	active pp.	passive pp.	gerund
end (intransitive)	**telë-**	telë	téla	**telë, teli-**	teluva	telenë	etélië	á telë	telela	télina	telië
end, cease	**tyel-**	tyelë	tyéla	tyelë, tyeli-	tyeluva	tyellë	etyélië	á tyelë	tyélala	tyelda	tyelië
entrap (in a net)	**remba-**	remba	rembëa	remba	rembuva	rembanë	erembië	á remba	rembala	rembaina	rembië
escape	**us-**	usë	úsa	**usë, usi-**	usuva	**ussë, úsë**	ustúsië, úsië	á usë	úsala	úsina	usië
establish, fix	**tulca-**	tulca	tulcëa	tulca	tulcuva	tulcanë	utulcië	á tulca	tulca	tulcaina	tulcië
exist, be	**ëa**	ëa		ëa		**engë**		ëa!			
expire, die	**effir-**	effírë	effíra	effírë	effíruva	effírnë	effírië	á effírë	effírala	effírma	**effírië**
fade	**sinta-**	sinta	sintëa	sinta	sintuva	**sintanë**	isintië	á sinta	sintala	sintaina	sintië
fade	**vinda-**	vinda	vindëa	vinda	vinduva	**vindanë**	ivindië, vindië	á vinda	vindala	vindaina	vindië
fade	**vinta-**	vinta	vintëa	vinta	vintuva	**vintë, vintanë**	ivintië, vintië	á vinta	vintala	vintaina	vintië
fade, die	**fir-**	fírë	fíra	**fírë, firi-**	fíruva	fírnë	ifírië, **fírië**	á fírë	fírala	fírma	firië
fail	**quel-**	quelë	quéla	quelë, queli-	**queluva**	quellë	equélië	á quelë	quelala	quelda	quelië
fall	**lanta-**	lanta	lantëa	lanta	lantuva	**lantanë**	alantië, **lantië**	á lanta	**lantala**	lantaina	lantië

Presented by http://www.ambar-eldaron.com

definition	verbal stem	infinitive	present	aoriste	future	past	perfect	imperative	active pp.	passive pp.	gerund
fall down, slip	talat-	talatë	talata	talatë, talati-	talatuva	talantë	atalatië	á talatë	talatala	talataina	talatië
fall in, collapse	atalta-	atalta	ataltëa	atalta	ataltuva	ataltanë	atáltië	á atalta	ataltala	ataltaina	ataltië
fashion, do	tan-	tanë	tána	tanë, tani-	tanuva	tannë	atanië	á tanë	tánala	tanna	tanië
fasten	tac-	tacë	táca	tacë, taci-	tacuva	tancë	atácië	á tacë	tácala	tácina	tacië
fear (+ablative)	ruc-	rucë	rúca	rucë, ruci-	rucuva	runcë	urúcië	á rucë	rúcala	rúcina	rucië
feel	fel-	felë	féla	felë, feli-	feluva	fellë	efelië	á felë	félala	felda	felië
feel disgust at, abhor	feuya-	feuya	feuyëa	feuya	feuyuva	feuyanë	eféwië	á feuya	feuyala	feuyaina	feuië
fetch, summon	tulta-	tulta	tultëa	tulta	tultuva	tultanë	utultië	á tulta	tultala	tultaina	tultië
fill	quat-	quatë	quáta	quatë, quati-	quantuva	quantë	aquátië	á quatë	quátala	quátina,	quatië
find	hir-	hirë	híra	hirë, hiri-	hiruva	hirnë	ihirië	á hirë	hirala	hirna	hirië
find	tuv-	tuvë	túva	tuvë, tuvi-	tuvuva	túvë	utúvië	á tuvë	túvala	túvina	tuvië
fix, establish	tulca-	tulca	tulcëa	tulca	tulcuva	tulcanë	utulcië	á tulca	tulca	tulcaina	tulcië
fix, set	panya-	panya	panyëa	panya	panyuva	panyanë	apánië	á panya	panyala	panyaina	panië

definition	verbal stem	infinitive	present	aoriste	future	past	perfect	imperative	active pp.	passive pp.	gerund
float, flow	**lutta-**	lutta	luttëa	lutta	luttuva	luttanë	uluttië	á lutta	luttala	luttaina	luttië
float, flow	**lutu-**	luto	lútua	lutui	lutúva	lutunë	ulútië	á luto	lutúla	lutuina	lutië
flood	**luita-**	luita	luitëa	luita	luituva	luitanë	uluitië	á luita	luitala	luitaina	luitië
flood	**oloiya-**	oloiya	oloiyëa	oloiya	oloiyuva	oloiyanë	olóilië	á oloiya	oloiyala	oloyaina	óloië
flow	**sir-**	sirë	síra	sirë, siri-	siruva	simë	isírië	á sirë	sírala	sirna	sirië
flow, float	**lutta-**	lutta	luttëa	lutta	luttuva	luttanë	uluttië	á lutta	luttala	luttaina	luttië
flow, float	**lutu-**	luto	lútua	lutui	lutúva	lutunë	ulútië	á luto	lutúla	lutuina	lutië
fly	**vil-**	vile	vila	**vilë, vili-**	viluva	**villë**	ivilië, vílië	á vilë	vilala	vilda	vilië
fly	**wil-**	wilë	wíla	**wilë, wili-**	wiluva	**willë**	iwílië, wílië	á wilë	wílala	wilda	wilië
fly (take refuge)	**ruc-**	rucë	rúca	**rucë, ruci-**	rucuva	runcë	urúcië	árucë	rúcala	rúcina	rucië
fly or stream in the wind, blow	**hlapu-**	hlapo	hlápua	hlapui	hlapíva	hlapunë	ahlápië	á hlapo	**hlápula**	hlapuina	hlapië
fly up	***amavil-**	amavilë	amávila	amavilë, amavili-	amaviluva	amavillë	ahamavilië	á amavilë	amavilala	amavilda	amavilië
fly up	***amawil-**	amawilë	amáwila	amawilë, amawili-	amawiluva	amawillë	ahamiwilië	á amawilë	amawilala	amawilda	amawilië

definition	verbal stem	infinitive	present	aoriste	future	past	perfect	imperative	active pp.	passive pp.	gerund
foam	**falasta-**	falasta	falastëa	falasta	falastuva	falastanë	afálastië	á falasta	**falastala**	falastaina	falastië
follow	**hilya-**	hilya	hilyëa	hilya	hilyuva	hilyanë	ihlië	á hilya	hilyala	hilyaina	hilië
follow, serve	**veuya-**	veuya	veuyëa	veuya	veuyuva	veuyanë	evéwië	á veuya	veuyala	veyuina	vevië
force, press, thrust	**nir-**	nirë	nira	**nirë, niri-**	niruva	**nindë**	inirmië	á nira	nirala	nirna	nirië
forge	**maca-**	maca	mácëa	maca	macuva	macanë	amácië	á maca	mácala	macaina	macië
forgive	**avatyar-**+ablatif	avatyarë	avatyara	avatyarë	avatyaruva	avatyaranë	avatyarië	**á avatyarë, ávatyarë**	avatyarala	avatyarma	avatyarië
forgive (+dative of person forgiven)	**apsene-**	apsenë	apsénëa	apsenë	apsenuva	apsennë	apsénië	á apsenë	apsénala	apseneina	apsenië
free	**rúna-**	rúna	rúnëa	rúna	rúnuva	rúnanë	urúnië	á rúna	rúnala	rúnaina	rínië
frost	**hel-**	helë	hélä	helë, heli-	heluva	hellë	ehelië	á helë	hélala	helda	helië
gather, collect	**hosta-**	hosta	hostëa	hosta	hostuva	hostanë	ohostië	á hosta	hostala	**hostaina**	hostie
get old	**yerya-**	yerya	yeryëa	yerya	yeryuva	yemë	eyérië	á yerya	yeryala	yeryaina	yerië
girate, swirl	**hwinya-**	hwinya	hwinyëa	hwinya	hwinyuva	hwinnë	ihwínië	á hwinya	hwinyala	hwinyaina	hwinië-
give	**anta-**	anta	antëa	anta	antuva	antanë, ánë	ántië, anántië	á anta	antala	antaina	antië

definition	verbal stem	infinitive	present	aoriste	future	past	perfect	imperative	active pp.	passive pp.	gerund
give thanks, thank	**hanta-**	hanta	hantëa	hanta	hantuva	hantanë	ahantië	á hanta	hantala	hantaina	hantië
gleam (white)	**ilca-**	ilca	ilcëa	ilca	ilcuva	ilcanë	ililcië, ilcië	á ilca	**ilcala**	ilcaina	ilcië
glint	**tin-**	tinë	tína	**tinë, tini-**	tinuva	tinnë	itinië	á tinë	tinala	tinna	tinië
glitter	**mirilya-**	mirilya	mirilyëa	mirilya	mirilyuva	mirillë	imirilië	á mirilya	mirilyala	mirilyaina	mirilië
go	**lenna-**	lenna	lennëa	lenna	lennuva	**lendë**	elennië	á lenna	lennala	lennaina	lennië
go away, leave	**auta- /1**	auta	autëa	auta	autuva	**anwë, vánë**	avánië	á auta	autala	vanwa	autië
go round, return	**pel-**	pelë	péla	pelë, peli-	peluva	pellë	epélië	á pelë	pélala	pelda	pelië
go, proceed	**lelya-**	lelya	lelyëa	lelya	lelyuva	**lendë**	elélië, lendië	á lelya	lelyala	lelyaina	lelië
govern	**tur-**	turë	túra	turë, turi-	turuva	turnë	utúrië	á turë	túrala	turna	turië
grasp	**mapa-**	mapa	mapëa	mapa	mapuva	mapanë, mampë	amápië	á mapa	mapala	mapaina	mapië
grow	**ol-**	olë	óla	olë, oli-	oluva	ollë	ololië, olië	á olë	ólala	olda	olië
growl, snarl	**yarra-**	yarra	yarrëa	yarra	yarruva	yarranë	ayarrië	á yarra	yarrala	yarraina	yarrië
grumble, murmur	**nurru-**	nurro	nurrua	nurrui	nurrúva	nurrunë	unurrië	á nurro	nurrula	nurruina	nurrië

definition	verbal stem	infinitive	present	aoriste	future	past	perfect	imperative	active pp.	passive pp.	gerund
guess, suppose	intya-	intya	intyëa	intya	intyuva	intyanë	inintië, intië	á intya	intyala	intyaina	intië
hallow	airita-	airita	airitëa	airita	airituva	airitánë	ahairitië	á airita	airitala	airitaina	airitië
hammer	namba-	namba	nambëa	namba	nambuva	nambanë	anambië	á namba	nambala	nambaina	nambië
hang, dangle	linga-	linga	lingëa	linga	linguva	linganë	ilingië	á linga	lingala	lingaina	lingië
harp	nanda-	nanda	nandëa	nanda	nanduva	nandanë	anandië	á nanda	nandala	nandaina	nandië
harp	tanta-	tanta	tantëa	tanta	tantuva	tantanë	atantië	á tanta	tantala	tantaina	tantië
hate	tevë-	tevë	téva	tevë, tevi-	tevuva	tévenë	etévië	á tevë	tevala	tévina	tevië
have an impulse, be compelled to do	horya-	horya	horyëa	horya	horyuva	hornë	ohórië	á horya	horyala	horyaina	horië
have, possess	harya-	harya	haryëa	harya	haryuva	harnë	ahárië	á harya	tévala	haryaina	harië
heal, renew	envinyata-	envinyata	envinyatëa	envinyata	envinyatuva	envinyatánë	envinyatië	á envinyata	envinyatála	envinyanta	envinyatië
hear	hlar-	hlarë	hlára	hlarë, hlari-	hlaruva	hlarnë	ahlárië	á hlarë	hlárala	hlarna	hlarië
hear	ten-	tenë	téna	tenë, teni-	tenuva	tennë	eténië	á tenë	tenala	tenna	tenië
heave	amorta-	amorta	amortëa	amorta	amortuva	amortanë	ámortië, amámortië	á amorta	amortala	amortaina	amortië

definition	verbal stem	infinitive	present	aoriste	future	past	perfect	imperative	active pp.	passive pp.	gerund
heave (intransitive, of heavy things)	**rúma-**	rúma	rúmëa	rúma	rúmuva	rúmanë	urúmië	á rúma	**rúmala**	rúmaina	rúmië
heed	**cim-**	cimë	címa	cimë, cimi-	cimuva	cimnë	icímië	á cimë	címala	cimna	cimië
hew	**pelecta-**	pelecta	pelectëa	pelecta	pelectuva	pelectanë	epélectië	á pelecta	pelectala	pelectaina	pelectië
hew	**pelehta-**	pelehta	pelehtëa	pelehta	pelehtuva	pelehtanë	epélehtië	á pelehta	pelehtala	pelehtaina	pelehtië
hew (with sword)	**mac-**	macë	máca	**macë, maci-**	macuva	mancë	amácië	á macë	mácala	mácina	macië
hide	**lom-**	lomë	lóma	**lomë, lomi-**	lomuva	lomnë	olómië	á lomë	lómala	lomna	lomië
hide	**moru-**	moro	mórua	morwë	morúva	morunë	omórië	á moro	morúla	moruina	morië
hide	**nurta-**	nurta	nurtëa	nurta	nurtuva	nurtanë	unurtië	á nurta	nurtala	nurtaina	nurtië
hint, wink	**huita-**	huita	huitëa	huita	huituva	huitanë	uhuitië	á huita	huitala	huitina	huitië
hold	**hep-**	hepë	hépa	hepë, hepi-	hepuva	hempë	ehempië	á hepë	hépela	hepina	hepië
hollow out	**unca-**	unca	uncëa	unca	uncuva	uncanë	uhuncië, huncië	á unca	uncala	uncaina	uncië
howl	**húna-**	húna	húnëa	húna	húnuva	húnanë	uhúnië	á húna	húnala	húnaina	húnië
hunt	**rauta-**	rauta	rautëa	rauta	rautuva	rautanë	arautië	á rauta	rautala	rautaina	rautië

definition	verbal stem	infinitive	present	aoriste	future	past	perfect	imperative	active pp.	passive pp.	gerund
hunt, pursue	**roita-**	roita	roitëa	roita	roituva	roitanë	oroitië	á roita	roitala	roitaina	roitië
illuminate-	**calya-**	calya	calyëa	calya	calyuva	calyanë	acálië	á calya	calyala	calyaina	calië
imagine, conceive	**nauta-**	nauta	nautëa	nauta	nautuva	nautanë	anautië	á nauta	nautala	nautaina	nautië
impel (impersonal)	**or- + datif**	orë	óra	**orë, ori-**	**oruva**	**oranë, ornë**	orórië, órië	á ora	órala	orna	orië
impel (impersonal)	**ora-**	ora	**órëa**	**ora**	**oruva**	**oranë, ornë**	orórië, órië	a ora	órala	oraina	**orië**
indicate	**tëa-**		tëa			**tengë**					
indicate, show	**tana-**	tana	tanëa	tana	tanuva	tananë	atánië	á tana	tanala	tanaina	tanië
induce	**sahta-**	sahta	sahtëa	sahta	sahtuva	sahtanë	asahtië	á sahta	sahtala	sahtaina	**sahtië**
insert	**mitta-**	mitta	mittëa	mitta	mittuva	mittanë	imittië	á mitta	mittala	mittaina	mittië
invent, originate	**auta-/3**	auta	autëa	auta	autuva	**autanë**	avánië	á auta	autala	vanwa	autië
it happens (impersonnal)	**marta-**	marta	martëa	marta	martuva	martanë	amartië	á marta	martala	martaina	martië
jerk	**rihta-**	rihta	rihtëa	rihta	rihtuva	rihtanë	irihtië	á rihta	rihtala	rihtaina	rihtië
judge	**ham-**	hamë	háma	**hamë, hami-**	hamuva	hamnë	ahámië	á hamë	hámala	hamna	hamië

definition	verbal stem	infinitive	present	aoriste	future	past	perfect	imperative	active pp.	passive pp.	gerund
judge	**nam-**	namë	náma	**namë, nami-**	namuva	namnë	anámië	ánamë	námala	namna	namië
judge	**nav-**	navë	náva	**navë, navi-**	navuva	navë	anávië	á navë	navala	navina	navië
jump	**cap-**	capë	cápa	capë, capi-	capuva	campë	acápië	á capë	cápala	cápina	capië
kill, murder	**qualta-**	qualta	qualtëa	qualta	qualtuva	qualtanë	aqualtië	á qualta	qualtala	qualtaina	qualtië
kindel	**tintila-**	tintila	tintilëa	**tintila**	tintiluva	tintilanë	itintilië	á tintila	tintila	tintilaina	tintilië
kindle	**narta-**	narta	nartëa	narta	nartuva	nartanë	anartië	á narta	nartala	nartaina	nartië
kindle	**turu-**	turo	túrua	turwë, turwi-	turúva	turuë	utúrië	á turo	turúla	turuina	turië
kindle (set light to)	**calta-**	calta	caltëa	calta	caltuva	caltanë	acaltië	á calta	caltala	caltaina	caltië
knock	**tamba-**	tamba	tambëa	tamba	tambuva	tambanë	atambië	á tamba	tambala	tambaina	tambië
knock, strike	**pet-**	petë	péta	petë, peti-	petuva	**pentë**	epetië	á petë	pétala	pétaina	petië
know about, understand	**hanya-**	hanya	hanyëa	hanya	hanyuva	hanyanë	ahánië	á hanya	haryala	hanyaina	hanië
labour	**móta-**	móta	mótëa	móta	mótuva	mótanë	omótië	á móta	mótala	mótaina	mótië
lament	**naina-**	naina	nainëa	naina	nainuva	nainanë	anánië	á naina	nainala	nainaina	nainië

definition	verbal stem	infinitive	present	aoriste	future	past	perfect	imperative	active pp.	passive pp.	gerund
lament	**nainaina-**	nainaina	nainainëa	nainaina	nainainuva	nainainë	ananainimë	á nainaina	nainainala	nainainaina / nainainimë	nainainimë
lament	**nyéna-**	nyéna	nyénëa	nyéna	nyénuva	nyénanë	enyénië	á nyéna	nyénala	nyénaina	nyénië
laugh	**lala-**	lala	lálëa	lala	láluva	lalanë, landë	alálië	á lala	lálala	lalaina	lalië
lead	**tulya- + allatif**	tulya	tulyëa	tulya	tulyuva	tulyanë	utúlië	á tulya	tulyala	tulyaina	tulië
lead	**mittanya- (+allatif)**	mittanya	mittanyëa	mittanya	mittanyuva	mittanyanë	imittanië	á mittanya	mittanyala	mittanyaina / mittanië	mittanië
leap	**halta-**	halta	haltëa	halta	haltuva	haltanë	ahaltië	á halta	haltala	haltaina	haltië
leave	**lesta-**	lesta	lestëa	lesta	lestuva	**lendë**	elestië	á lesta	lestala	lestaina	lestië
leave physically	**auta- /2**	auta	autëa	auta	autuva	**oantë**	oantië	á auta	autala	vanwa	autië
leave, go away	**auta- /1**	auta	autëa	auta	autuva	**anwë, vánë**	avánië	á auta	autala	vanwa	autië
lessen	**pica-**	pica	picëa	pica	picuva	picanë	ipícië	á pica	**pícala**	picaina	picië
let go, let loose, free	**sen-**	senë	séna	senë, sem-	senuva	senne	esénië	á senë	sénala	senna	semë
let loose, free, let go	**sen-**	senë	séna	senë, sem-	senuva	senne	esénië	á senë	sénala	senna	semë
lick	**lav-**	lave	láva	**lavë, lavi-**	lavuva	**lávë**	alávië	á lavë	lávala	lávina	lavië

definition	verbal stem	infinitive	present	aoriste	future	past	perfect	imperative	active pp.	passive pp.	gerund
lick	**sulp-**	sulpë	sulpa	sulpë, sulpi-	sulpuva	sulppë	usulpië	á sulpë	sulpala	sulpina	sulpië
lick (frequentative)	**lapsa-**	lapsa	lapsëa	lapsa	lapsuva	lapsanë	alapsië	á lapsa	lapsala	lapsaina	lapsië
lick up, sup, sip	**salpa-**	salpa	salpëa	salpa	salpuva	salpanë	asalpië	á salpa	salpala	salpaina	salpië
lie (horizontally)	**caita-**	**caita**	caitëa	caita	caituva	**cainä, cäante**	acaitië	á caita	caitala	caitaina	caitië
lie heavy	**lumna-**	lumna	lumnëa	lumna	lumnuva	**luvë**	ulumnië	á lumna	lumnala	lumnaina	lumnië
lie, conceal	**fur-**	furë	fúra	furë, furi-	furuva	furnë	ufúrië	á furë	furala	furna	furië
lie, conceal	**hur-**	hurë	húra	hurë, huri-	huruva	hurnë	uhúrië	á hurë	húrala	hurna	hurië
linger	**lenda-**	lenda	lendëa	lenda	lenduva	lendanë	elendië, **lendië**	á lenda	lendala	lendaina	lendië
listen	**lasta-**	lasta	lastëa	lasta	lastuva	lastanë	alastië	á lasta	lastala	lastaina	lastië
live	***cuil-**	cuilë	cuila	cuilë, cuili-	cuiluva	cuillë	ucuilië	á cuilë	cuilala	cuilda	cuilië
loathe, abhor	**yelta-**	yelta	yeltëa	yelta	yeltuva	yeltanë	eyeltië	á yelta	yeltala	yeltaina	yeltië
long for	**milya-**	milya	milyëa	milya	milyuva	milyanë	imfilië	á milya	milyala	milyaina	milië
look at	**yéta-**	yéta	yétëa	yéta	yétuva	yétanë	eyétië	á yéta	yétala	yétaina	yétië

definition	verbal stem	infinitive	present	aoriste	future	past	perfect	imperative	active pp.	passive pp.	gerund
look for, pursue	**saca-** /1	saca	sacëa	saca	sacuva	**sácë**	asácië	á saca	sacala	sacaina	sacië
loose, slacken	**lehta-**	lehta	lehtëa	lehta	lehtuva	lehtanë	elehtië	á lehta	lehtala	lehtaina	lehtië
loose, slacken	**lenca-**	lenca	lencëa	lenca	lencuva	lencanë	elencië	á lenca	lencala	lencaina	lencië
love	**mel-**	melë	méla	melë, meli-	meluva	mellë	emélië	á melë	mélala	melda	melië
lower, brood	**luvu-**	luvo	lúvua	luvui	lúviva	luvunë	ulúvië	á luvo	luvúla	luvuina	luvië
make	**cen-**	cenë	céna	cenë, ceni-	**cenuva**	cennë	ecénië	á cena	cénala	cenna	cenië
make a twang, twang	**tinga-**	tinga	tingëa	tinga	tinguva	tinguva	itingië	á tinga	tingala	tingaina	tingië
make flat	**lara-**	lara	larëa	lara	laruva	laranë	alarië	á lara	larala	laraina	larië
make network or lace	**raita-** /1	raita	raitëa	raita	raituva	raitanë	araitië	á raita	raitala	raitaina	raitië
make network or lace	**rëa-**	rëa		rëa		rengë		rëa!			
make spin, stir	**quir-**	quirë	quíra	quirë, quiri-	quiruva	**quindë**	iquitië	á quirë	quírala	quírma	quitië
mar	**hasta-**	hasta	hastëa	hasta	hastuva	hastanë	ahastië	á hasta	hastala	**hastaina**	hastië
murder, kill	**qualta-**	qualta	qualtëa	qualta	qualtuva	qualtanë	aqualtië	á qualta	qualtala	qualtaina	qualtië

definition	verbal stem	infinitive	present	aoriste	future	past	perfect	imperative	active pp.	passive pp.	gerund
murmur, grumble	**nurru-**	nurro	nurrua	nurrui	nurrúva	nurrunë	unurrië	á nurro	nurrula	nurruina	nurrië
name	**esta-**	esta	estëa	esta	estuva	estanë	ehestië, estië	á esta	estala	estaina	estië
not allow to, stop	**nuhta-**	nuhta	muhtëa	nuhta	nuhtuva	nuhtanë	unuhtië	á nuhta	nuhtala	nuhtaina	nuhtië
not be, not do	**um-**	umë	umëa	umë, umi-	úva	**úmë**	uhúmië, húmië	á umë	umela	umna	umië
not do, not be	**um-**	umë	umëa	umë, umi-	úva	**úmë**	uhúmië, húmië	á umë	umela	umna	umië
not to do	**hum-**	humë	húma	**humë, humi-**	humuva	**húmë**	uhúmië	á huma	humala	humna	humië
open	**latya-**	latya	latyëa	latya	latyuva	latyanë	alátië	á latya	latyala	latyaina	latië
open wide	**palu-**	palo	pálua	palwë, palwi-	palíva	palunë	apálië	á palo	palúla	paluina	palië
open wide, spread	**palya-**	palya	palyëa	palya	palyuva	palyanë	apálië	á palya	palyala	palyaina	palië
open, unfurl	**panta-**	panta	pantëa	panta	pantuva	pantanë	apantië	á panta	pantala	pantaina	pantië
order, command	**can-**	canë	cána	canë, cani-	canuva	cannë	acánië	á canë	cánala	canna	canië
originate, invent	**auta- /3**	auta	autëa	auta	autuva	**autanë**	avánië	á auta	autala	vanwa	autië
overshadow	**telta-**	telta	teltëa	telta	teltuva	teltanë	eteltië	á telta	teltala	teltaina	teltië

Presented by http://www.ambar-eldaron.com

definition	verbal stem	infinitive	present	aoriste	future	past	perfect	imperative	active pp.	passive pp.	gerund
pain, torment	**nwalya-**	nwalya	nwalyëa	nwalya	nwalyuva	nwalyanë	anwálië	á nwalya	nwalyala	nwalyaina	nwalië
pick up with fingers	**lepta-**	lepta	leptëa	lepta	leptuva	leptanë	eleptië	á lepta	leptala	leptaina	leptië
plant	**empanya-**	empanya	empanyëa	empanya	empanyuva	**empannë**	empánië	á empanya	empanyala	empanyaina	empanië
play	**tyal-**	tyalë	tyála	**tyalë, tyali-**	tyaluva	tyallë	atyálië	á tyalë	tyálala	tyalda	tyalië
possess, have	**harya-**	harya	haryëa	harya	haryuva	harnë	ahárië	á harya	tévala	haryaina	harië
pour (intransitive)	**ulya-**	ulya	úlëa	ulya	ulyuva	**ullë**	ulúlië, ulië	á ulya	ulyala	ulyaina	ulië
pour (transitive)	**ulya-**	ulya	úlëa	ulya	ulyuva	**ulyanë,**	ulúlië, ulië	á ulya	ulyala	ulyaina	ulië
pout	**penga-**	penga	pengëa	penga	penguva	penganë	epengië	á penga	pengala	pengaina	pengië
pray	**arca-**	arca	arcëa	arca	arcuva	arcanë	árcië	á arca	arcala	arcaina	arcië
pray	**hyam-**	hyamë	hyama	**hyamë, hyami-**	hyamuva	hyamnë	ahyámië	á hyama	hyamala	hyamma	hyamië
prepare	**manwa-**	manwa	manwëa	manwa	manwuva	manwanë	amanwië	á manwa	manwala	manwaina	manwië
press, force, thrust	**nir-**	nirë	níra	**nirë, niri-**	niruva	**nindë**	inirië	á nira	nirala	nirma	nirië
prick	**erca-**	erca	ercëa	erca	ercuva	ercanë	ercië, erercië	á erca	ercala	ercaina	ercië

definition	verbal stem	infinitive	present	aoriste	future	past	perfect	imperative	active pp.	passive pp.	gerund
prick, sting	**nasta-**	nasta	nastëa	nasta	nastuva	nastanë	anastië	á nasta	nastala	nastaina	nastië
proceed, go	**lelya-**	lelya	lelyëa	lelya	lelyuva	**lendë**	elélië, lendië	á lelya	lelyala	lelyaina	lelië
prohibit, refuse	**áva-**	áva	ávëa	ava	avuva	**avanë**	ávië, avávië	**áva**	avala	avaina	avië
prolong	**taita-**	taita	taitëa	taita	taituva	taitanë	atáitië	á taita	taitala	taitaina	taitië
protect	**varya-**	varya	varyëa	varya	varyuva	varyanë	avárië, várië	á varya	varyala	varna	varie
puff	**hwesta-**	hwesta	hwestëa	hwesta	hwestuva	hwestanë	ehwestië	á hwesta	hwestala	hwestaina	hwestië
pull, draw	**saca- /2**	saca	sacëa	saca	sacuva	**sácë**	asácië	á saca	sacala	sacaina	sacië
pursue, hunt	**roita-**	roita	roitëa	roita	roituva	roitanë	oroitië	á roita	roitala	roitaina	roitië
pursue, look for	**saca- /1**	saca	sacëa	saca	sacuva	**sácë**	asácië	á saca	sacala	sacaina	sacië
put an end to	**metya-**	metya	metyëa	metya	metyuva	metyanë	emétië	á metya	metyala	metyaina	metië
put aside, abandon	**hehta-**	hehta	hehtëa	hehta	hehtuva	**hehtanë**	ehehtië	á hehta	hehtala	hehtaina	hehtië
put shame, abuse	**naitya-**	naitya	naityëa	naitya	naituva	naityanë	anaitië	á naitya	naityala	naityaina	naitië
quarrel	**costa-**	costa	costëa	costa	costuva	costanë	ocostië	á costa	costala	costaina	costië

definition	verbal stem	infinitive	present	aoriste	future	past	perfect	imperative	active pp.	passive pp.	gerund
raise	**amu-**	amo	ámua	amwë, amwi-	amúva	amunë	ámië, amámië	á amo	amúla	amuina	amië
raise, rise	**orta-**	orta	ortëa	orta	ortuva	**ortanë**	orortië, ortië	á orta	ortala	ortaina	ortie
reach, strech out	**racta-**	racta	ractëa	racta	ractuva	ractanë	aractië	á racta	ractala	ractaina	ractië
reach, strech out	**rahta-**	rahta	rahtëa	rahta	rahtuva	rahtanë	arahtië	á rahta	rahtala	rahtaina	rahtië
receive	**cam-**	camë	cáma	camë, cami-	camuva	**camnë**	cámië	á camë	camala	camaina	camië
receive	**tuvu-**	tuvo	túvua	tuvui	tuvúva	tuvunë	utúvië	á tuvo	tuvúla	tuvuina	tuvië
reckon	**not-**	note	nóta	note, noti-	notuva	nontë	onótië	á notë	nótala	**nótina**	notië
refill	**enquat-**	enquatë	enquáta	enquatë, enquati-	**enquantuva**	enquantë	enquátië	á enquatë	enquátala	enquátina	enquatië
reflect, think	**sana-**	sana	sanëa	sana	sanuva	sananë	asánië	á sana	sánala	sanaina	sanië
refuse, prohibit	**áva-**	áva	ávëa	ava	avuva	**avanë**	ávië, ávávië	**áva**	avala	avaina	avië
refuse, say no	**avaquet-**	avaquetë	avaquéta	avaquetë, avaqueti-	avaquetuva	avaquetë	avaquetië	á avaquetë	avaquétala	avaquetina	avaquetië
refuse, say no	**váquet-**	váquetë	váquéta	**váquetë, váqueti-**	váquetuva	**váquetë**	aváquétië, vaquetië	á váquetë	váquétala	váquetina	váquetië
release	**lerya-**	lerya	leryëa	lerya	leryuva	leryanë	elérië	á lerya	leryala	leryaina	lerië

Presented by http://www.ambar-eldaron.com

definition	verbal stem	infinitive	present	aoriste	future	past	perfect	imperative	active pp.	passive pp.	gerund
remain	**er-**	erë	éra	erë, eri-	eruva	ernë	ehernië	á erë	erala	erna	erië
remain, tarry	**lemya-**	lemya	lemyëa	lemya	lemyuva	lemyanë	elémië	á lemya	lemyala	lemyaina	lemië
rend	**narca-**	narca	narcëa	narca	narcuva	narcanë	anarcië	á narca	narcala	narcaina	narcië
renew	**enyal-**	enyalë	enyála	enyalë, enyali	enyaluva	enyallë	enayálië	á enyala	enyalala	enyalla	**enyalië**
renew, heal	**envinyata-**	envinyata	envinyatëa	envinyata	envinyatuva	envinyatánë	envinyatië	á envinyata	envinyatála	**envinyanta**	envinyatië
rest	**ser-**	serë	séra	serë, sen-	seruva	**sendë**	esérië	á serë	serala	serna	senë
return, come back	**entul-**	entulë	entúla	entulë, entuli-	entuluva	entullë	entúlië	á entulë	entulala	entulda	entulië
returngo, round	**pel-**	pelë	péla	pelë, peli-	peluva	pellë	epélië	á pelë	pélala	pelda	pelië
rise, raise	**orta-**	orta	ortëa	orta	ortuva	**ortanë**	orortië, ortië	á orta	orala	ortaina	ortie
roof	**tópa-**	tópa	tópëa	tópa	tópuva	tópanë	otópië	á tópa	tópala	tópaina	tópaië
rule	**heru-**	hero	hérua	herwë, herwi-	herúva	herunë	ehérië	á hero	herúla	heruina	herië
rule (divine power)	**vala-**	vála	valëa	valë, vali-	**valuva**	valanë	aválië, válië	á vala	válala	valaina	valië
run	**yur-**	yurë	yúra	**yurë, yuri-**	yuruva	yurnë	uyúrië	á yurë	yurala	yurna	yurië

definition	verbal stem	infinitive	present	aoriste	future	past	perfect	imperative	active pp.	passive pp.	gerund
run on, run smoothly	**nornoro-??**	nornoro	nornorëa	nornorë, nornori-	nornoruva	nornoronë	onornorië	á nornoro	nornórola	nornoroina	nornorië
sail	**círa-**	círa	círëa	círa	círuva	círanë	icirië	á círa	círala	círaina	círië
say	**quet-**	quetë	quëta	quetë, queti-	quetuva	**quentë**	equétië	á quetë	quétala	quétina	quetië
say no, refuse	**avaquet-**	avaquetë	avaquéta	avaquetë, avaqueti-	avaquetuva	avaquentë	avaquetië	á avaquetë	avaquétala	avaquetina	avaquetië
say no, refuse	**váquet-**	váquetë	váquéta	**váquetë, váqueti-**	váquetuva	**váquentë**	aváquétië, váquetië	á váquetë	váquétala	váquetina	váquetië
scatter, blow about	**winta-**	winta	wintëa	winta	wintuva	wintanë	iwintië, wintië	á winta	wintala	wintaina	wintië
screen from the light, conceal	**halya-**	halya	halyëa	halya	halyuva	halyanë	ahálië	á halya	halyala	halyaina	halië
see	**vél-**	velë	véla	velë, veli-	véluva	vélanë	evélië, vélië	á véla	vélala	vélda	vélië
send	**lenta**	lenta	lentëa	lenta	lentuva	**lentanë**	elentië	á lenta	lentala	lentaina	lentië
send	**lelta-**	lelta	leltëa	lelta	leltuva	**leltanë**	eleltië	á lelta	leltala	leltaina	leltië
send, cause to go	**menta-**	menta	mentëa	menta	mentuva	mentanë	ementië	á menta	mentala	mentaina	mentië
serve, follow	**veuya-**	veuya	veuyëa	veuya	veuyuva	veuyanë	evéwië	á veuya	veuyala	veyuina	vevië
set (of the sun)	**numenda-**	númenda	númendëa	númenda	númenduva	númendanë	unúmendië	á númenda	númendala	númendaina	númendië

definition	verbal stem	infinitive	present	aoriste	future	past	perfect	imperative	active pp.	passive pp.	gerund
Set (of the sun)	**númeta-**	númeta	númetëa	númeta	númetuva	númetanë	umímetië	á númeta	númetala	númetaina	númetië
set aside	**sat-**	satë	sáta	satë, sati-	satuva	santë	asatië	á satë	sátala	sátina	satië
set, fix	**panya-**	panya	panyëa	panya	panyuva	panyanë	apánië	á panya	panyala	panyaina	panië
set, sink (Sun or Moon)	**núta-**	núta	nútëa	núta	nútuva	nútanë	umútië	á nuta	nútala	nutaina	nutië
shine	**cal-**	calë	cála	calë, cali-	**caluva**	callë	acálië	á calë	cálala	calda	calië
shine (white)	**ninquita-**	ninquita	ninquitëa	ninquita	ninquituva	ninquitanë	ininquitië	á ninquita	ninquitala	ninquitaina	ninquitië
shine (white) freq.	**sisila-**	sisila	sisilëa	sisila	sisiluva	sisilanë	isisilië	á sisila	**sisilala**	sisilaina	sisilië
shine (with white light)	**sil-**	silë	**síla**	**silë, sili-**	siluva	sillë	isílië	á silë	silala	silda	silië
shout	**rama-**	rama	rámëa	rama	ramuva	ramanë	arámië	á rama	rámala	ramaina	ramië
show, indicate	**tana-**	tana	tanëa	tana	tanuva	tananë	atánië	á tana	tanala	tanaina	tanië
sin	**úcar-**	úcarë	úcára	**úcarë, úcari-**	úcaruva	úcarnë	úcarië, *úacarië	á úcarë	úcarala	úcarna, úcarina	úcarië
sing	**linda-**	linda	lindëa	linda	linduva	lindanë	ilindië	á linda	lindala	lindaina	lindië
sing	**lir-**	lire	líra	**lirë, liri-**	liruva	lirmë	ilirië	á lire	lirala	lirma	lirië

definition	verbal stem	infinitive	present	aoriste	future	past	perfect	imperative	active pp.	passive pp.	gerund
sink, set (Sun or Moon)	**núta-**	núta	nútëa	núta	nútuva	nútanë	umútië	á nuta	nútala	nutaina	nutië
sip, lick up, sup	**salpa-**	salpa	salpëa	salpa	salpuva	salpanë	asalpië	á salpa	salpala	salpaina	salpië
sit	**ham-**	hamë	háma	**hamë, hami-**	hamuva	hamnë	ahámië	á hamë	hámala	hamna	hamië
sit	**har-**	harë	**hára**	harë, hari-	haruva	**handë**	ahárië	á harë	hárala	harna	harië
slacken, loose	**lehta-**	lehta	lehtëa	lehta	lehtuva	lehtanë	elehtië	á lehta	lehtala	lehtaina	lehtië
slacken, loose	**lenca-**	lenca	lencëa	lenca	lencuva	lencanë	elencië	á lenca	lencala	lencaina	lencië
slay	**nahta-**	nahta	nahtëa	nahta	nahtuva	nahtanë	anahtië	á nahta	nahtala	**nahtana,** nahtaina	nahtië
slide down, collapse	**talta-**	talta	taltëa	talta	taltuva	taltanë	ataltië	á talta	**taltala**	taltaina	taltië
slip, fall down	**talat-**	talatë	talata	talatë, talati-	talatuva	talantë	atalatië	á talatë	talatala	talataina	talatië
slowly fade away	**fifíru-**	fifíro	fifírua	fifírui	fifírúva	fifírúnë	ifífírië	á fifíro	**fifírula**	fifíruina	fifírië
slumber	**lor-**	lorë	lóra	lorë, lori-	loruva	lornë	olórië	á lorë	lórala	lorna	lorië
slumber	**muru-**	muro	múrua	murwë, murwi-	murúva	murunë	umúrië	á muro	murúla	muruina	murië
snare	**rem-**	remë	réma	**remë, remi-**	remuva	remmë	erémië	á remë	remala	remna	remië

definition	verbal stem	infinitive	present	aoriste	future	past	perfect	imperative	active pp.	passive pp.	gerund
snarl, growl	**yarra-**	yarra	yarrëa	yarra	yarruva	yarranë	ayarrië	á yarra	yarrala	yarraina	yarrië
snow	**fauta-**	fautë	fauta	fauta	fautuva	fauntë	afautië	á fautë	fautala	fautina	fautië
sound	**lamya-**	lamya	lamya	lamya	lamyuva	lamnë	alámië	á lamya	lamyala	lamyaina	lamië
sow	**rer-**	rerë	réra	**rerë, reri-**	reruva	**rendë**	erérië	árerë	rérala	rerna	rerië
sparkle	**ita-**	ita	itëa	ita	ituva	itanë	ihitië, itië	á ita	itala	itaina	itië
sparkle	**tintina-**	tintina	tintinëa	tintina	tintinuva	tintinanë	itintinië	á tintina	tintinala	tintinaina	tintinië
speed, urge	**horta-**	horta	hortëa	horta	hortuva	hortanë	ohortië	á horta	hortala	hortaina	hortië
spin, turn	**pir-**	pirë	píra	pirë, piri-	piruva	pirnë	ipirië	á pirë	pirala	piraina	pirië
spit	**piuta-**	piuta	piutëa	piuta	piutuva	piutanë	ipiutië	á piuta	piutala	piutaina	piutië
spread, open wide	**palya-**	palya	palyëa	palya	palyuva	palyanë	apálië	á palya	palyala	palyaina	palië
sprout	**locta-**	locta	loctëa	locta	loctuva	loctanë	oloctië	á locta	loctala	loctaina	loctië
sprout	**lohta-**	lohta	lohtëa	lohta	lohtuva	lohtanë	olohtië	á lohta	lohtala	lohtaina	lohtië
sprout	**lohta-**	lohta	lohtëa	lohta	lohtuva	lohtanë	olohtië	á lohta	lohtala	lohtaina	lohtië

definition	verbal stem	infinitive	present	aoriste	future	past	perfect	imperative	active pp.	passive pp.	gerund
sprout	**tuia-**	tuia	tuiëa	tuia	tuiuva	tuianë	utúië	á tuia	tuiala	tuiaina	tuië
squat	**haca-**	haca	hácëa	haca	hacuva	hacanë	ahácië	á haca	hácala	hacaina	hacië
stain	**vahta-**	vahta	vahtëa	vahta	vahtuva	vahtanë	avahtië, vahtië	á vahta	vahtala	vahtaina	vahtië
stand up	**tyulta-**	tyulta	tyultëa	tyulta	tyultuva	tyultanë	utyultië	á tyulta	tyultala	tyultaina	tyultië
stick, abide by, adhere	**himya-**	himya	himyëa	himya	himyuva	himyanë	ihímië	á himya	himyala	himyaina	himië
sting, prick	**nasta-**	nasta	nastëa	nasta	nastuva	nastanë	anastië	á nasta	nastala	nastaina	nastië
stir, make spin	**quir-**	quirë	quira	quirë, quiri-	quiruva	**quindë**	iquitië	á quirë	quirala	quírma	quitië
stir, swarm	**uma-**	uma	umëa	uma	umuva	umanë	uhúmië	á uma	umala	umaina	umië
stop	**pusta-**	pusta	pustëa	pusta	pustuva	pustanë	upustië	á pusta	pustala	pustaina	pustië
stop, block	**tap-**	tape	tápa	**tapë, tapi-**	tapuva	**tampë**	atápië	á tape	tapala	tápina	tapie
stop, cease, take rest	**hauta-**	hauta	hautëa	hauta	hautuva	hautanë	ahautië	á hauta	hautala	hautaina	hautië
stop, not allow to	**nuhta-**	nuhta	nuhtëa	nuhta	nuhtuva	nuhtanë	unuhtië	á nuhta	nuhtala	nuhtaina	nuhtië
stray	**ranya-**	ranya	ranyëa	ranya	ranyuva	rannë	aránië	á ranya	ranyala	ranyaina	ranië

definition	verbal stem	infinitive	present	aoriste	future	past	perfect	imperative	active pp.	passive pp.	gerund
stray about	**mista-**	mista	mistëa	mista	mistuva	mistanë	imistië	á mista	mistala	mistaina	mistië
stream or fly in the wind, blow	**hlapu-**	hlapo	hlápua	hlapui	hlapúva	hlapunë	ahlápië	á hlapo	**hlápula**	hlapuina	hlapië
strech out, reach	**racta-**	racta	ractëa	racta	ractuva	ractanë	aractië	á racta	ractala	ractaina	ractië
strech out, reach	**rahta-**	rahta	rahtëa	rahta	rahtuva	rahtanë	arahtië	á rahta	rahtala	rahtaina	rahtië
stretch	**lenu-**	leno	lénua	lenwë, lenwi-	lenúva	lenunë	elénië	á leno	lenúla	lenuina	lenië
stride	**telconta-**	telconta	telcontëa	telconta	telcontuva	telcontanë	etelcontië	á telconta	telcontala	telcontaina	telcontië
strike, knock	**pet-**	petë	péta	petë, peti-	petuva	**pentë**	epetië	á petë	pétala	pétaina	petië
suffocate, choke	**quoro-??**	quoro	quorëa	quorë, quori-	quoruva	quoronë	oquoronië	á quoro	quórola	quoroina	quorië
summon	**naham-**	nahamë	naháma	nahamë, nahami-	nahamuva	nahamnë	anáhamië	á hahamë	nahámala	**nahamna**	nahamië
summon	**nahom-**	nahomë	nahóma	nahomë	nahomuva	nahomnë	anáhomië	á nahomë	nahómala	**nahomna**	nahomië
summon	**natyam-**	natyamë	natyáma	natyamë, natyami-	natyamuva	natyamnë	anatyamië	á natyamë	natyámala	**natyamna**	natyamië
summon	**yal-**	yalë	yála	yalë, yali-	yaluva	yallë	ayálië, yálië	á yalë	yálala	yalda	yalië
summon, fetch	**tulta-**	tulta	tultëa	tulta	tultuva	tultanë	utultië	á tulta	tultala	tultaina	tultië

definition	verbal stem	infinitive	present	aoriste	future	past	perfect	imperative	active pp.	passive pp.	gerund
sup, lick up, sip	salpa-	salpa	salpëa	salpa	salpuva	salpanë	asalpië	á salpa	salpala	salpaina	salpië
suppose	ista-	ista	istëa	ista	istuva	sintë	isintië, sintië	á ista	istala	istaina	istië
suppose, guess	intya-	intya	intyëa	intya	intyuva	intyanë	inintië, intië	á intya	intyala	intyaina	intië
swarm, stir	uma-	uma	umëa	uma	umuva	umanë	uhúmië	á uma	umala	umaina	umië
swell	tiuya-	tiuya	tiuyëa	tiuya	tiuyuva	tiunë	utúië	á tiuya	tiuyala	tiuyaina	tiuië?
swirl, girate	hwinya-	hwinya	hwinyëa	hwinya	hwinyuva	hwinnë	ihwinië	á hwinya	hwinyala	hwinyaina	hwinië-
take rest, cease, stop	hauta-	hauta	hautëa	hauta	hautuva	hautanë	ahautië	á hauta	hautala	hautaina	hautië
take vengeance	*atacar-	altacarë	altacára	altacarë, altacari-	altacaruva	altacarnë	ahalatacárië	á altacarë	altacárala	altacarna	altacarië
tangle	fasta-	fasta	fastëa	fasta	fastuva	fastanë	afastië	á fasta	fastala	fastaina	fastië
tap	tam-	tamë	táma	tamë, tami-	tamuva	tamnë	atámië	á tamë	tamala	tamna	tamië
tarry, remain	lemya-	lemya	lemyëa	lemya	lemyuva	lemyanë	elémië	á lemya	lemyala	lemyaina	lemië
taste	tyav-	tyavë	tyáva	tyavë, tyavi-	tyavuva	tyávë	atyávië	á tyavë	tyávala	tyávina	tyavië
teach	saita-	saita	saitëa	saita	saituva	saitanë	asaitië	á saita	saitala	saitaina	saitië

definition	verbal stem	infinitive	present	aoriste	future	past	perfect	imperative	active pp.	passive pp.	gerund
tell	**nyar-**	nyarë	nyára	**nyarë, nyri-**	nyaruva	nyarnë	anyárië	á nyarë	nyárala	nyarna	nyarië
terrify	**ruhta-**	ruhta	ruhtëa	ruhta	ruhtuva	ruhtanë	uruhtië	á ruhta	ruhta	ruhtaina	ruhtië
thank, give thanks	**hanta-**	hanta	hantëa	hanta	hantuva	hantanë	ahantië	á hanta	hantala	hantaina	hantië
think, reflect	**sana-**	sana	sanëa	sana	sanuva	sananë	asánië	á sana	sánala	sanaina	sanië
thrive	**al-**	alë	ála	alë, ali-	aluva	allë	álië, alálië	á alë	álala	alda	alië
thrive	**ala-**	ala	alëa	ala	aluva	alanë	álië, alálië	á ala	alala	alaina	alië
thrust, force, press	**nir-**	nirë	níra	**nirë, niri-**	niruva	**nindë**	inirnië	á nira	nirala	nirna	nirië
tie, bind	**nut-**	nutë	núta	**nutë, nuti-**	nutuva	nutnë	unútië	á nutë	nútala	nútina	nutië
tie, bind	**serta-**	serta	sertëa	serta	sertuva	**sérë**	esertië	á serta	sertala	sertaina	sertië
torment, pain	**nwalya-**	nwalya	nwalyëa	nwalya	nwalyuva	nwalyanë	anwálië	á nwalya	nwalyala	nwalyaina	nwalië
touch (literally)	**appa-**	appa	appëa	appa	appuva	appanë	áppië, appápië	á appa	appala	appaina	appië
trade	**manca-**	manca	mancëa	manca	mancuva	mancanë	amancië	á manca	mancala	mancaina	mancië
tremble	**papa-**	papa	papëa	papa	papuva	papanë, pampë	apapië	á papa	papala	papaina	papië

definition	verbal stem	infinitive	present	aoriste	future	past	perfect	imperative	active pp.	passive pp.	gerund
trim, adorn	netya-	netya	netyéa	netya	netyuva	netyanë	enétië	á netya	netyala	netyaina	netië
turn	quer-	querë	quéra	querë, queri-	queruva	quendë	equerië	á querië	querala	querna	querië
turn, spin	pir-	pirë	píra	pirë, piri-	piruva	pirnë	ipirië	á pirë	pirala	piraina	pirië
twang, make a twang	tinga-	tinga	tingëa	tinga	tinguva	tinguva	itingië	á tinga	tingala	tingaina	tingië
twinkle	tinta-	tinta	tintëa	tinta	tintuva	tintanë	itintië	á tinta	tintala	tintaina	tintië
twist	ric-	ricë	ríca	ricë, rici-	ricuva	rince	irícië	áricë	ricala	ricína	ricië
understand, know about	hanya-	hanya	hanyëa	hanya	hanyuva	hanyanë	ahánië	á hanya	haryala	hanyaina	hanië
unfurl, open	panta-	panta	pantëa	panta	pantuva	pantanë	apantië	á panta	pantala	pantaina	pantië
urge, speed	horta-	horta	hortëa	horta	hortuva	hortanë	ohortië	á horta	hortala	hortaina	hortië
use	yuhta-	yuhta	yuhtëa	yuhta	yuhtuva	yuhtanë	uyuhtië	á yuhta	yuhtala	yuhtaina	yuhtië
veil	vasarya-	vasarya	vasaryëa	vasarya	vasaryuva	vasaryanë	avásarië, vásarië	á vasarya	vasaryala	vasaryaina	vasarië
veil, cloak	fanta-	fanta	fantëa	fanta	fantuva	fantanë	afantië	á fanta	fantala	fantaina	fantië
wake up	eccoita-	eccoita	eccoitëa	eccoita	eccoituva	eccoitanë	eccoitië	á eccoita	eccoitala	eccoitaina	eccoitië

definition	verbal stem	infinitive	present	aoriste	future	past	perfect	imperative	active pp.	passive pp.	gerund
walk	**vanta-**	vanta	vantëa	vanta	vantuva	vantanë	avantië, vantië	á vanta	vantala	vantaina	vantië
war (make war upon)	**ohtacar-**	ohtacarë	ohtacára	ohtacarë,	ohtacaruva	**ohtacarnë**	ohohtacarië, ohtacárië	á ohtacarë	ohtacárala	ohtacarna	ohtacárië
warm	**lauta-**	lauta	lautëa	lauta	lautuva	lautanë	alautië	á lauta	lautala	lautaina	lautië
watch	**cenda-**	cenda	cendëa	cenda	cenduva	cendanë	ecendië	á cenda	cendala	cendaina	cendië
watch	**tir-**	tire	tíra	tirë, tiri-	**tiruva**	tirnë	itírië	**tira**, á tira	tirala	tirna	tirië
weave	**lanya-**	lanya	lanyëa	lanya	lanyuva	lanyanë	alánië	á lanya	lanyala	lanyaina	lanië
wed	**vesta-**	vesta	vestëa	vesta	vestuva	vestanë	evestië, vestië	á vesta	vestala	vestaina	vestië
whisper	**hlussa-**	hlussa	hlussëa	hlussa	hlussuva	hlussanë	uhlussië	á hlussa	hlussala	hlussaina	hlussië
whisper	**lussa-**	lus sa	lussëa	lussa	lussuva	lussanë	ulussië	á lussa	lussala	lussaina	lussië
whiten	**ninquitá-**	ninquitá	ninquitëa	ninquitá	ninquituva	ninquitanë	ininquitië	á ninquitá	ninquitala	ninquitaina	ninquitië
wield a weapon	**mahta-**	mahta	mahtëa	mahta	mahtuva	mahtanë	amahtië	á mahta	mahtala	mahtaina	mahtië
wink, hint	**huita-**	huita	huitëa	huita	huituva	huitanë	uhuitië	á huita	huitala	huitina	huitië
wish to go somewh.	**mina-**	mina	minea	mina	minuva	minane	iminië	a mina	minala	mmaina	minië

definition	verbal stem	infinitive	present	aoriste	future	past	perfect	imperative	active pp.	passive pp.	gerund
wound	**harna-**	harna	harnéa	harna	harnuva	harnanë	aharnië	á harna	harnala	**harna**	harnië
write	**tec-**	tecë	téca	**tecë, teci-**	tecuva	tencë	etécië	átecë	tecala	técina	tecië
yawn	**yanga-**	yanga	yangëa	yanga	yanguva	yanganë	ayangië, yangië	á yanga	yangala	yangaina	yangië